DAVENPORT HOUSE 7

DAVENPORT HOUSE 7

— HARD TIMES —

MARIE SILK

DAVENPORT HOUSE BOOKS BY MARIE SILK

PREQUEL
Davenport House
Debutante

BOOK ONE
Davenport House

BOOK TWO
Davenport House
A New Chapter

BOOK THREE
Davenport House
A Mother's Love

BOOK FOUR
Davenport House
Heiress Interrupted

BOOK FIVE
Davenport House
For the Cause

BOOK SIX
Davenport House
House Secrets

BOOK SEVEN
Davenport House
Hard Times

Chapter 1

"I think we should make up the ballroom for an indoor wedding, just in case the weather turns on us," Clara Davenport said decidedly at the dinner table. "What do you think, Joe?"

Clara's fiance, Joe Blake, turned to look at her as if he just snapped out of a daze. "What was the question, darling?" he asked.

"I said that I think we should set up the ballroom for our guests, in the event the weather makes an outdoor wedding impossible," Clara repeated. "We don't want to be rained out like poor Fiona was at her spring wedding."

Fiona, the housekeeper of Davenport House, was clearing dishes from the table just then and smiled to remember. "It was only a typical Irish wedding, Miss Clara," she joked. Everyone at the dinner table laughed—except for Mary Hamilton, who instead seemed to be staring curiously at Fiona.

"Always good to have a backup plan," Joe said in answer to Clara's question.

"Always," Clara said with a smile. "I only hope that

Abigail arrives in time for the dress fitting tomorrow. You'll be ready for your fitting in the morning, right Mary?"

Mary glanced away from Fiona. "Of course I will," she answered distractedly.

Clara looked back and forth between Mary and Fiona and waited until Fiona had left the dining room to ask. "Mary, what are you up to? Do you and Fiona have a surprise planned for my wedding? If so, you must tell me now. I don't want any surprises that day!"

Mary laughed. "We are not up to anything."

"Let them have their secrets, dear," Joe said to Clara. "Otherwise it won't be a surprise."

"It's nothing like that," Mary said, exchanging a knowing smile with her husband, Dr. William Hamilton, who sat across from her at the table. "I just think you may need to look for a new housekeeper soon."

Clara's face fell. "Has she mentioned something to you about leaving?"

Mary shook her head then leisurely sipped from her water glass. "She has not said a word to me about anything, Clara. It's just a feeling I have."

Clara gasped when she understood her meaning. Mary had worked as a midwife in the past and could usually detect when a woman was expecting. "Do you think she is...already?" Clara asked, but was interrupted by Fiona entering the room with dessert plates.

Everyone at the table was silent as she served the dessert. When she realized that all eyes seemed to be on her, Fiona stood up straight and smoothed her uniform. "Is there something I've forgotten to go with the dessert, Miss Clara?" she asked.

"No, the dessert is fine," Clara replied. She paused before

she continued carefully, "Mary just seems to think you might be leaving Davenport House—for some reason—in the future."

"Clara," Joe scolded quietly. "You'll embarrass the poor girl."

Fiona's face did turn red, but at the same time she felt relief that she need not bring up the subject herself. "I—I wasn't going to say anything until after your wedding, Miss Clara. You have so much to think about already."

Mary grinned and told her, "We are very happy for you and Sam."

"Thank you, Mrs. Hamilton. We are very happy too," Fiona grinned back.

Clara forced a smile. "You will be sorely missed here, but I am at least glad you will be happy."

"Thank you, Miss Clara. If I may be honest…we haven't told Abigail yet…we wanted to surprise her with the news when she comes tomorrow," Fiona explained.

"Of course," Mary replied. "Your secret is safe with us!"

Fiona blushed again and returned downstairs to the kitchen while the others finished their dessert.

After dinner, Mary and William excused themselves from the table and walked up the grand staircase of the stately mansion. "I hope Violet went to sleep this time," Mary sighed as they went up the stairs. "She did not sleep at all last night. I don't know what I'd do without Serena here to help me."

William looked at her apologetically. "I'm sorry I haven't been home much lately."

"I understand that your patients need you too," said Mary. "I should be fine with Serena's help."

"There's something I wanted to tell you, but I wasn't sure if I should say so at dinner," William said.

"What is it?"

William took a deep breath. "There are rumors of a new doctor setting up his practice in town."

"Oh?" Mary said, raising her eyebrows. "Does it mean you might be able to come home more often?"

William smiled. "It's why I mentioned it. The only thing is, no one knows who the new doctor will be. It's still rumor at this point. But do you remember the mercantile that was closed recently and how I said it would be a fine building to expand the clinic? It's just been taken off the market and there is talk of it being converted to a hospital. I don't know what this will mean for the clinic."

"I see," Mary replied thoughtfully. "I haven't heard anything about a new hospital, just that poor Mrs. Spencer lost her income when she closed the mercantile. Who told you about the new doctor?"

William cringed. "I'm ashamed to admit that I read about it in the paper's new gossip column."

Mary's mouth fell open. "William, I never would have guessed you read that silly thing! The rumor probably isn't true, then. I would hardly call anything that comes out in that column newsworthy."

"And how would you even know whether anything it says is newsworthy?" William teased her.

"I don't read it on purpose," she assured him with a laugh. "Clara forces me to listen every morning at tea. She was out of town with the florist this morning so that must be why I never heard about the rumored doctor."

They reached their bedroom door and Mary gently pushed it open. Serena Valenti, the neighbor who helped care for their baby, was crocheting in a rocking chair near the fireplace. The quiet room was lit only by firelight. Serena stood up from the rocking chair and motioned to the cradle. "Violet has been sleeping all this while," she whispered.

Mary put her hand over her heart and breathed in relief. "Oh, I'm so glad. Thank you, Serena."

Serena nodded and gathered her crocheting supplies. "Goodnight, Mary. Goodnight, Dr. Hamilton." She left the room and closed the door.

William and Mary stood over the cradle, gazing upon their baby sleeping peacefully before them. "I will never tire of watching her sleep," said Mary. "She is so perfect and innocent. Sometimes when I look at her, I have this strange buildup of feelings…it almost feels like a rage."

William chuckled. "I don't understand how looking at our precious daughter could invite such feelings."

"It just makes me so angry to think that someday, someone might hurt her. The rage comes from thoughts of what I would do to anyone who tries."

"It must be your maternal instinct. I feel the same way, Mary. Heaven help the man who stands between us and our child."

While William and Mary were retiring to bed, Clara spoke with Joe in the gardens behind the house. Joe's cottage was located on the neighboring estate and he usually walked home through the gardens after dinner. "I will miss you," Clara said to him as they embraced. "I can't wait until you never have to leave again. We can simply retire upstairs like William and Mary."

Joe smiled and kissed her cheek. "You only have one more week to wait, my darling."

Clara sighed thoughtfully. "And now I must think of where to find a new housekeeper. Can you believe that Fiona is with child at a time like this?"

"It happens, Clara," Joe said with a chuckle. "I'm certain it will be us soon enough."

Clara was suddenly nervous. "Joe, there is something I need to tell you, only I haven't known how to say it."

"All right, I'm listening."

Clara looked down at the ground. "I went to the doctor for some problems I was having many months ago. I was too embarrassed to ask William or Mary about it, so I went to a clinic in Philadelphia instead. The doctor told me that I might be past my time to have children."

Joe looked at her sadly. "I didn't realize. I'm sorry, Clara."

"But we can still be happy, can't we? Just you and me together," Clara said hopefully. "This doesn't change your mind, does it?"

Joe smiled down at her. "Of course not. With as many friends as you have, I'm sure the house will always be full of children anyway."

Clara hugged him tighter. "I was hoping you would understand."

"Clara," he whispered. "It's getting late. I should be going home."

She backed away from him and smiled. "I suppose you're right. See you at dinner tomorrow?"

Joe shook his head. "I have to go to Harrisburg to settle some business. I don't know how long it will take, but I may miss dinner."

"Oh that's right," Clara remembered. "But I will see you at dinner the day after?"

"Of course. Goodnight, darling."

"Goodnight, Joe."

The next morning at Davenport House, the maids prepared a room for Abigail and Ethan Smith, who were coming to visit with their toddler boy. Abigail was going to be a matron of honor in Clara's upcoming wedding, along with Mary, Clara's best friend.

It was about the time that Abigail promised to arrive for the dress fitting. The seamstress was already in the house and had the bridesmaid dresses laid out on the beds. Mary heard the sound of a car coming up the drive and went outside to see if it was William. Her mouth dropped open when she realized that the car parking in front of the house had Ethan behind the wheel and Abigail smiling beside him.

"Whose car is this?" Mary exclaimed.

Ethan laughed as he walked around the front to open Abigail's door. "It's mine."

"I don't believe it! I thought surely you would come riding in with the carriage. I even had Sam prepare the stable for your horses," replied Mary. "Good morning, Abigail. Oh! Here is my darling nephew!"

Abigail held little Patrick on her hip as she approached Mary. "Good morning," she greeted cheerfully. "Can you please take him while I get some of my things out of the back?"

Mary hesitated. "Um, is Patrick walking yet? I could hold his hand and take him into the house."

"Yes, he is walking now," Abigail said, setting the toddler down on the grass.

"I'll take our things inside," Ethan told them. "You go on ahead and get reacquainted. I'm sure Clara has plenty for you to do anyway," he added with a wry grin.

Just then, Clara stepped outside in a fluster and began speaking very fast. "Oh good, you're here Abigail. The seamstress is inside with the dresses and ready to see them on you ladies. I was just now going to tell Serena that the dresses are here. Oh Ethan, since you are here, you can go tell Serena. I have to make another phone call to the florist." Clara disappeared back into the house.

"I knew she'd put me to work with wedding stuff as soon as we got here," Ethan mumbled while he collected the luggage.

"And you're such a good sport about it," Mary said, putting her arms around him and kissing his cheek. "It is good to see you, dear brother."

"It's good to see you too." He followed the ladies inside with the luggage, then left the house to visit the Valenti family who lived in a farmhouse nearby.

"Hello," Phillip Valenti greeted. He was working in the garden when he saw Ethan approaching. "I didn't know you were back in town."

"Just got here," Ethan replied. "Clara sent me over to get Serena."

"Then it must be regarding the big day," Phillip chuckled.

"I suppose. She said something about dresses." Ethan looked over the sparse vegetable garden that Phillip was working in. "Did you have trouble with the crops this year?"

Phillip shook his head in frustration. "It's been so dry, and I've been out in town looking for work so I guess I didn't tend to the gardens as much as I should have."

"What kind of work are you looking for?"

"Anything, really. Most jobs are taken as soon as they come available. I'm not the only soldier looking for odd jobs," said Phillip. "I might need to go to the big city to find something permanent."

"I'll send word if I hear anything open up in Philadelphia, but the situation is similar there," said Ethan.

Phillip nodded and stood to his feet, wiping the dirt from his hands on his work pants. "I sure would appreciate if you could let me know. I'll go inside and tell Serena that Clara needs her."

Back at Davenport House, Mary and Abigail were looking at their new dresses laid out on the bed in Mary's room. "I'm afraid that mine will be too tight," Mary said quietly. "I don't think it will fit."

Abigail looked at Mary's dress and then at Mary. "It looks about right. I'm sure it will be no trouble to alter if it needs more room."

But Mary seemed reluctant to even touch the bridesmaid dress. "Why don't you try yours on first?" she said.

Abigail nodded and changed into the pink ruffled dress. She looked at herself in the full length mirror and cringed. "It certainly has a lot of bows," she said quietly. She turned around to face Mary. "How do I look?" Mary was frowning. "Is it that awful?" Abigail questioned, pulling at some of the pink bows.

"No, it's not that. I'm just worried about this part here," she said, pointing below Abigail's waist. "I think it will be too painful for me to wear—against my scar."

Abigail looked at Mary compassionately when she remembered that she had birthed by a Cesarean operation. "Oh I'm sorry, Mary. I had forgotten about that. You are still in pain?"

Mary became downcast. "Sometimes the pain is so bad that I can barely hold Violet in my arms. It pains me to lift anything. I feel helpless most of the time."

"That's why you seemed hesitant today when I asked if you could take Patrick," Abigail said.

"Yes, I was afraid to lift him. Serena comes to the

house to help me daily. If she did not, I don't know what I would do."

"What does William say about it? Is there anything that can be done?"

"No. I mean, I haven't said much to him about it. Honestly Abigail, I think something must have gone wrong during the operation and I don't want William to feel badly about it."

"I see. I will help you into the dress but I'll be very careful about closing the back. You can tell me if it starts to hurt. Should we try it?"

Mary agreed and let Abigail help her into the new dress. She gasped in pain when she felt the dress against her waist. "Stop! It's too tight!" she cried while quickly stepping out of the dress. Tears began streaming down her face.

Abigail was in disbelief. "Mary, I hadn't even begun to close the dress in the back. Are you worried I might pull it too tight? I promise I'll be careful."

"You don't understand," Mary whimpered. "It was already too painful."

Abigail frowned. "Then I'm worried you might have an infection. The incision should have healed by now. Will you let me have a look?"

Mary covered her face with her hands. "I've seen it in the mirror. It looks terrible. I certainly don't want William to see me while I look like this."

"Please, Mary. You have me very concerned now," Abigail persisted.

Mary lay back on the bed and pulled up her slip to reveal the scar under her belly. Abigail appeared perplexed as she examined her. "I told you it looks terrible," Mary said.

"It's not infected, and that's the important thing. I

just don't understand why the bruising doesn't appear to have healed by now. Your birth was so many months ago but your healing is not making the progress it should. No wonder you are in so much pain. You should speak to William about it as soon as you see him again."

Mary carefully put her slip back down and sat up on the bed. "What will I do about the wedding? Clara will be upset if I can't wear the dress."

Abigail looked at the dress again. "I can take the material out here so the front hangs down loosely like the clothes you have been wearing. Do you think it could work if I did so?"

"Yes, as long as it's not pressing me along the front."

"It will be no trouble at all to change the dress—but Mary, I really think you should be resting more so you can recover properly. I will do everything I can to help with Violet during my visit."

"You're an angel," Mary said in relief. "Thank you."

CHAPTER 2

Phillip Valenti returned to his farmhouse after a hard day's work. His sister Serena arrived about the same time as he. "Are you just now getting home?" she asked him.

"I picked up an extra job, but it was further than my usual ones," he answered, opening the front door for her. Phillip became alarmed by the smell of smoke when they entered the farmhouse. He rushed to the kitchen where the rug in front of the stove was just beginning to erupt into flames. A burning ember had fallen through the open firebox door of the cook stove. Phillip quickly threw the rug into the kitchen sink. "Gabriella!" he shouted angrily to summon his ten year old daughter. "Gabriella Maria!"

"Thank goodness we got here when we did!" Serena exclaimed. She went to the bedrooms to find the children, but they were not there. Gabriella was in charge of her younger brother Donnie and her cousin Angelina while the adults were away. Serena found all three children playing outside. "Gabriella, go to your papa in the kitchen," she said sternly, then swooped Angelina into her arms and kissed her. "Thank goodness everyone is all right."

Gabriella skipped inside the house at first, but her face fell when she smelled the smoke and saw her father's face red with anger.

Phillip pointed to the firebox on the cook stove. "How many times do I have to tell you to never leave the kitchen with that door open?"

"I forgot," she whimpered.

"Because you weren't paying attention!" he yelled. "You could have burned the whole house down! Then where would we live?"

Gabriella thought for a moment. "We could live with grandma and grandpa," she answered innocently.

Phillip grew angrier at the thought of it. "We have to take care of our own house or we'll sleep on the street. Would you like that?"

Gabriella hung her head. "No. I'm sorry, Papa."

" 'Sorry' doesn't mend the rug or keep the house from burning down," he grumbled as he removed the rug from the sink, which had become covered in soot. "Now clean up this mess."

Gabriella nodded mournfully and rolled up her sleeves to wash out the sink. Serena returned into the house and shook her head at Phillip. "She is only a child," she scolded him quietly. "You expect too much of her."

Phillip shrugged. "It's for her own good. I'm already worried sick all day that something like this will happen when neither you nor I are home. Gabriella needs to grow up and be responsible if we're to have any chance of making it!"

"But you looked upset even before you walked into the house," Serena remarked. "What happened in town?"

"I have to pay taxes on the farmhouse by the end of summer. They won't give me any more time past that, but I can barely afford to feed us each week. I may have to sell the farmhouse and move us back to the city."

"I didn't realize it was so dire," Serena said with a frown. "How much do you need for the tax? You can have all the money I've saved."

"It's not enough," he told her. "I'm behind a few years' worth on the taxes. I thought things would be better by now, but they're only getting worse."

"I'm sorry, brother," she said helplessly. "Where will we go?"

"I'm still trying to figure that out," he mumbled, then retired to his bedroom for the night.

The next afternoon at Davenport House, Clara, Mary, and Abigail were having tea in the sitting room. Abigail cringed while Clara read the gossip column aloud to them. That day's article suggested that the mayor's wife, who prided herself on her exquisitely styled hair, actually wore a wig the whole time.

"I wouldn't be surprised if the mayor shuts down the paper after that article," Mary stated, shaking her head.

"It's why the journalist remains anonymous," Clara said, folding the paper and placing it on the table. "No one in their right mind could put their name to such a piece. Oh, I suppose I shouldn't be reading this now anyway. I have too much to do today!"

"What are your plans, Clara?" Abigail asked her. "Anything that Mary and I can help with?"

"The dress for my flower girl will be delivered shortly so I'll be visiting the Valentis to be sure it fits Gabriella. I also must speak with Joe about the place settings for the wedding guests. Oh dear, I nearly forgot about putting an ad in the newspaper for a new housekeeper. We're already short on staff with only Jane and Fiona, and I'm afraid Jane is too timid and doesn't have the experience to manage the whole house. Could Fiona have picked a more busy time to get pregnant?"

Abigail stifled a giggle. "Mary and I will help with the search for a housekeeper while you attend to the wedding details, Clara."

"Oh thank you," Clara said in relief.

Just then, Fiona entered the room. "A parcel has arrived for you, Miss Clara."

"Thank you, Fiona. Stay with me please while I see which parcel it is," replied Clara. She turned to Mary and Abigail. "That is probably Gabriella's dress. I had better go. I'll see you two at dinner."

Clara went down the grand staircase and saw a rectangular box wrapped with ribbon on the entry table. "Yes, this is the flower girl dress," she mentioned to Fiona, who followed her down the stairs. "I will be back in a little while."

"Very good, Miss Clara," Fiona replied. She brought Clara her hat and shawl and Clara left with the box for the Valentis' farmhouse.

"Hello Clara," Phillip greeted her at the door. "Serena isn't here just now."

"I have come to see your daughter. Her dress is here and I want to be sure it fits properly," Clara said, holding up the box. "Thank you for letting Gabriella be part of the wedding."

"I think she is looking forward to getting out of the house for once," he said with a chuckle. "Gabriella is in her room down the hall if you'd like to surprise her with it."

Clara nodded and took the box with her down the hallway. She peered through the open door and saw Gabriella sitting on the bed. "Good afternoon, dear," Clara said gently.

Gabriella looked up. "Miss Clara?"

Clara could see her tear stained cheeks. "Whatever is the matter?"

Gabriella hung her head. "Papa is angry with me because I almost burned down the house."

"Oh dear," Clara replied. She did not know how to respond, so she changed the subject. "What do you suppose I have in this box?"

Gabriella shrugged, but her eyes grew wide with wonder.

"It's your flower girl dress," Clara announced proudly. She untied the ribbon and opened the box while Gabriella watched intently. Clara pulled the dress out and held it up for her to see. "What do you think?"

"But it doesn't look like a flower at all! It's a party dress!"

Clara laughed. "Why did you think it would look like a flower?"

"You said I was going to wear a dress that would make me a flower girl," Gabriella answered. "But this is much better."

"Now let's be sure it fits. You will be wearing it on Saturday for the wedding."

Gabriella nodded and let Clara help her into the dress. "I hope Saturday comes soon," she said with a grin, running her hands down the pink ruffles.

Clara smiled and stroked the little girl's cheek. "I hope so too. I can't wait! But for now, we'll need to put the party dress in your Aunt Serena's room for safekeeping until the wedding."

"All right," Gabriella agreed. She removed the dress and gave it back to Clara.

Clara left Gabriella's room and placed the box on Serena's bed. She saw Phillip again in the kitchen on her way out. "I have good news. The dress fits perfectly," she said with a smile. "What did Gabriella mean by almost burning down the house?"

Phillip groaned "She left the firebox to the cook stove open."

"Oh dear, that will do it," Clara said. She looked past him at the cook stove. "But Phillip, this stove is ancient. Is it truly what you've been cooking on all this while?"

"I'm afraid so," he replied. "Can't afford a new one anytime soon."

"But it's a fire hazard in itself. When was the last time you cleaned the chimney?"

Phillip looked sheepish. "I don't remember."

"Then you must do so right away. My mother used to make me clean the kitchen chimney at Davenport House when I was younger. The buildup inside can be dreadful."

"Sometimes I forget you used to work as a maid at the grand house," Phillip said. "It must be very different now."

"There are some days it feels like a lifetime ago, but others that it feels like only yesterday," Clara reminisced. "I miss my mother most of all. I wish she could see me now and attend my dream wedding."

"I heard that your mother was a great lady," Phillip said. "You certainly take after her. Joe is a fortunate man."

"I will tell him you said so," Clara said with a grin as she headed for the door. "I want to be sure he knows it!"

In the city of Yorktown, Abigail and Mary were on their way to visit the office of the local newspaper. They had written an ad in search of a new housekeeper for Clara. "I hope we can find the perfect candidate for the house. Fiona did a lovely job, but I'm not sure Clara thought anyone could live up to the standards her mother set out," Abigail remarked.

"Mrs. Price is sorely missed at the house," Mary said quietly. "How did you choose your housekeeper for the manor house?"

"It wasn't very difficult. She was the head nurse while the house was used as a hospital for the Red Cross. She already knew the house inside and out—it only made sense to hire her when the time came for us to move back in. It still feels strange for Ethan and I to employ a servant at all. But I don't think I could keep up after the whole house, especially now that I have Patrick. Ethan tends to all of the horses, of course, but we'll often hire soldiers to help around the estate. They are terribly in need of employment now that the War is over."

The ladies stopped walking when they saw the line of men standing outside the employment office. "Mary, what is happening? The line is worse today than I've ever seen it," Abigail mentioned sadly.

"I never realized it was this bad," Mary whispered. "Oh look, it's Mrs. Spencer from the mercantile. It seems she is giving out pastries to the men in line. Poor Mrs. Spencer. Her husband died in the War and she recently had to close up their store altogether. She said that people just stopped buying. I suppose everyone is running out of money."

"It is kind of her to feed the soldiers today," Abigail said. "Let's see if she needs any help."

Mrs. Spencer was grateful to have the help. She directed the ladies to her carriage where several boxes of items were left. Abigail and Mary handed out baked goods and soup tins until the boxes were empty. Phillip Valenti stood toward the back of the line and accepted the gifts gratefully from Abigail. "Be sure to tell Mrs. Spencer I said 'thank you'. The children will enjoy these," he said.

"Of course I will tell her," Abigail promised. "How are the children?"

"They're all right." Phillip looked at the line ahead of him in discouragement. "I guess I should start walking home now. I don't imagine the employment office will still be open by the time they get to me."

"I'm sorry, Phillip. Mary and I will give you a ride home. We drove here in the car."

Phillip looked relieved. "I sure would appreciate that. Thank you."

Meanwhile, Mrs. Spencer spoke with Mary near the carriage. "I'm afraid this is the last of my inventory," Mrs. Spencer told her. "When I saw all the men waiting here for hours outside, I thought they could use something sweet to keep 'em going. I'm only sorry I won't have anything more to give after today."

"What will you do now that the mercantile is closed?" asked Mary.

Mrs. Spencer sighed. "I suppose I'll keep praying for the Lord to provide. The mercantile wasn't only my job, it was my home too. Once I paid the bank after the sale, there wasn't much left over for me to live on. But I do feel guilty looking for a job now when all these soldiers are looking too."

Mary paused while she considered what to say. "Abigail and I came to town today to place an ad in the paper for a new housekeeper. I wonder, how might you feel about keeping up with a forty room mansion? I will put in a good word for you with the Mistress, of course, if you would consider it."

"Would you really? Thank you, Mrs. Hamilton! I've never run a large house before, but I know how to work long hours and manage a business. A house can't be too much different, can it? I will certainly do my best!" Mrs. Spencer answered with newfound hope in her eyes.

Mary smiled with excitement. "Then I will put this advertisement back in my purse for now and speak to Clara about it tonight."

Later that evening, Clara, Abigail, Mary, William, and Ethan were dressed for dinner and waiting in the drawing room. Mary told Clara about the encounter with Mrs. Spencer.

Clara perked up. "Oh, I do hope Mrs. Spencer will take the job. It would take all the stress out of searching. She has a calming presence, doesn't she?"

"Indeed she does," agreed Abigail. "I am glad we ran into her today. It must have been meant to be."

"I'll ask Fiona to begin training her as soon as possible," Clara decided. "I'm sure Joe will be agreeable to Mrs. Spencer as our new housekeeper." She looked up at the clock as she had many times that evening, then turned her gaze to the vacant seat beside her where Joe usually sat before dinner. The others waited patiently and continued to converse, but Clara noticed them stealing glances at the clock too. She sighed reluctantly. "Let us go in to dinner. It appears that Joe will be a little late today. Fiona can show him in when he arrives."

The others gratefully rose from their seats and went into the dining room. While they dined that night, Clara could not help but stare in disappointment at her fiance's empty place setting at the table. The place setting remained empty for the rest of the night.

The next day, Clara rose early and put her shawl around her shoulders for a walk in the cool morning air. She went to Joe's cottage on the neighboring estate and knocked on the door. "Joe?" she called. There was no answer. Joe never locked his door, so Clara knocked one more time before turning the doorknob and peering into the house. Everything was quiet inside the cottage. The fireplace was cold and there was no sign of Joe. Feeling discouraged, Clara walked out of the house and closed the door. She was startled by a voice behind her.

"Miss Clara?"

Clara turned to see Sam, her own groundskeeper. "Sam? What are you doing here?"

"Mr. Blake asked if I could look after the livestock while he went to Harrisburg. He said it would just be for a day, but the cows got out this morning so I came to see if he got back. Do you know if he'll be gone much longer?"

Clara shrugged helplessly. "I expected Joe to return two nights ago but he must have been delayed. Do you mind tending to the livestock just a little longer?"

"It's no trouble, Miss Clara," Sam answered.

"Thank you, Sam. And congratulations on the little one you and Fiona are expecting. I think we may have found a new housekeeper, so it shouldn't be much longer that Fiona has to work at the house. Here, why don't you take this. I was going to give Joe the leftovers from last night's dinner." She handed him the knapsack she carried.

Sam gladly accepted it. "Thank you, Miss Clara. I hope the new housekeeper works out good for you."

Clara returned to the house where Mary and Abigail were already seated at the breakfast table. "Oh, did you go out this morning?" Mary asked her.

"I went to see Joe and take him the leftovers from last night's dinner. Apparently he has still not returned from his visit to Harrisburg. Have either of you heard the telephone ring? He surely would have called if he was going to be delayed this long."

"I'm sorry, Clara. I haven't heard the phone ring, but Mary and I were in town for most of yesterday," said Abigail.

"Oh that's right," Clara answered. "I'm beginning to feel worried. The wedding rehearsal is the day after tomorrow. Joe's suit is still at the tailor's."

"Perhaps you can telephone Joe's hotel in Harrisburg," Mary suggested.

"He didn't give me the name of the hotel he was staying at," Clara said, her look of concern growing worse. "Perhaps he did tell me the name and I was so caught up with everything else that I forgot."

Abigail smiled at Clara. "Mary and I will be sure to hear if the phone rings today. More than likely, Joe is on his way right now and will be home any moment."

Clara nodded and tried to smile too. "Thank you, Abigail. I'm sure he will be."

Chapter 3

"Brother! You will never believe who sent us a parcel!" Serena Valenti exclaimed when she walked through the door of the farmhouse. "Can you guess?"

Phillip was cooking soup on the kitchen stove and turned to look at her. "I give up."

"Oh, you are no fun. It's from our parents!" she squealed. "I wonder what's inside!"

Phillip stared at her in disbelief. "How would our parents know this address?"

Serena opened the parcel while she explained. "I sent our mother a letter to tell her of the terrible ordeal I had in finding Angelina. I never expected to hear back, but—oh how lovely! Look, it's a quilt for the children." When Serena lifted the quilt from the parcel, an envelope fell onto the floor near Phillip's feet. Serena looked at Phillip expectantly and waited for him to pick it up, but he turned around and stirred the soup instead.

Serena rolled her eyes and picked up the envelope herself. "If you weren't so stubborn, you might have been happy to see there is cash in this envelope."

Phillip didn't turn around. "What do they want?" he mumbled.

Serena read over the letter. "The money is train fare for you, me, and all the children to visit them in Pittsburgh. Oh I can't believe it! Mother writes that she wants me and Angelina to move back into their home!"

"What does our father think about all this?" Phillip questioned skeptically.

"Does it matter? I'm being invited back into our family home!" she said, tears forming in her eyes. "We must leave directly after the wedding."

" 'We'? I'm not going back to Pittsburgh with you."

"I know you're angry with them for my sake, but clearly they are trying to make things right. Mother writes that she has been plagued with guilt since she heard of Angelina's kidnapping, and she is sorry she ever forced me to leave the house."

"She should be sorry," Phillip responded. "Angelina could very well have died in the hands of those people."

"Well I am taking Angelina to Pittsburgh with or without you. I'll explain to Mary tonight."

"Suit yourself," Phillip said, then returned to his soup on the stove top.

At Davenport House, Mrs. Spencer arrived to receive training in the duties of housekeeper. Clara met her in the main Hall.

"Thank you for the chance to be housekeeper here, Miss Clara," Mrs. Spencer said humbly. "I will do my best to live up to the great housekeepers who came before me."

"I am certain you will do just as well," Clara said with a smile. "This is Fiona. She will show you the house and everything you need to know. Fiona will be leaving us about the same time I leave for my honeymoon. You will have plenty of time to familiarize yourself with the house and the routine while my husband and I are away."

"Yes, Madam," Mrs. Spencer nodded.

"Fiona, please notify me when the man from the telephone company arrives. And be sure to bring me anything that comes in the post immediately," instructed Clara.

"Yes, Miss Clara," Fiona responded. She led Mrs. Spencer on a tour through the house and was sure not to mention the subject which seemed to hang over the house like a dark cloud—the fact that Joe Blake had still not returned.

Fiona took Mrs. Spencer down the servants' stairs to the kitchen. "I will introduce you to our cook and housemaid. Ideally, the house will have two maids at all times, but we only have Jane for now. It means the workload is heavy for Jane and I, especially with the wedding. I imagine that Miss Clara will not want to wait much longer for a second maid once Mr. Blake moves into the house. When you do hire a new maid, she can help in the kitchen as well as with the other rooms."

"Is the cook making all the food for the wedding?" asked Mrs. Spencer.

"Mrs. Malone is making some of the food, but because we are understaffed, Miss Clara has hired outside catering for the wedding dinner."

Mrs. Spencer nodded along as she tried to remember the details. Fiona introduced her to the housemaid Jane and Mrs. Malone, the cook. She then took her up the servants' stairs to the third floor. "This is where the family bedrooms are. Dr. and Mrs. Hamilton live here, although Dr. Hamilton isn't home much. Ethan and Abigail are here for only a short while. Miss Mary and Abigail are sisters-in-law because Ethan is Miss Mary's brother. Abigail is also my sister-in-law since her brother is my husband, Sam."

"I'm not sure I'll be able to remember how everyone here is related," Mrs. Spencer said timidly.

Fiona giggled. "It was very complicated to me at first, but it begins to make sense once you have been here for a while." Fiona noticed that Mrs. Spencer seemed perplexed. "Do you have a question?"

"I'm just wondering…how did Miss Clara become Mistress of the house? Wasn't her mother the housekeeper? And shouldn't Miss Mary have been the heiress after Mr. Davenport passed away?"

Fiona sighed. "Mrs. Spencer, you are asking questions to which even I don't fully understand the answers. I think it's probably best to do my work without thinking too hard about it, and leave the rest of it up to the family."

Mrs. Spencer nodded. "Of course. Then I will do the same."

"I think you should help Mrs. Malone in the kitchen for today. Goodness knows she needs it since she has already begun on the wedding food. Did you know the rehearsal is tomorrow evening?"

"I do now," laughed Mrs. Spencer.

Fiona was glad that the new housekeeper was a woman of good nature. She had the sort of pleasing laugh that made anyone in her presence feel at ease. "Yes, it is indeed tomorrow," Fiona confirmed. "The rehearsal will take place upstairs in the ballroom. Jane and I will spend the rest of today setting it up." A ringing sound was heard just then.

"Is that the telephone?" asked Mrs. Spencer.

"No, that is the doorbell. I believe it's the man from the

telephone company. Miss Clara asked him to come by to ensure that our telephone is functioning properly. I must go answer the door now and notify Miss Clara of his arrival."

Mrs. Spencer nodded. "I will return downstairs and help Mrs. Malone with the food."

Fiona greeted the man at the door and showed him to the library where the telephone was located. Clara was already there waiting for him. "My telephone doesn't seem to be working properly," she told him. "I believe that someone has been trying to call me but is unable to ring through."

"I'm happy to have a look, Ma'am," the man told her. Just then, the telephone rang loudly and startled them both.

"Hello?" Clara answered it in a fluster.

"Hello Clara, it's William. Is Mary there?"

Clara slouched in disappointment and held the mouthpiece away so she could talk to Fiona. "It is William calling for Mary."

Fiona nodded and went upstairs to tell Mary.

"Telephone seems to be working fine, Ma'am. I'll be leaving now unless you need me for anything else," the man told her.

"Wait! Is it possible that only some calls are coming through properly, but not others?" she asked.

"It doesn't work like that, Ma'am. I'm sorry," he replied.

"Thank you for your time," she said in defeat. Clara left the library to show him the way out.

Mary found the library empty when she arrived downstairs. She picked up the telephone receiver from the desk. "William? Are you still there?"

"I'm here, Mary," said William's voice. "I did as you asked and spoke to the hospitals along the way from here to Harrisburg. None of them have seen Joe."

Mary sighed in relief. "Well I guess that's good news in a way…isn't it?"

"It's good news that no one has found him hurt, or worse. When was he due back?"

"Three days ago, and still not a word from him," Mary answered quietly.

"I'm sorry, Mary. You might try the police station next."

"I'll do so if he is still not back by tomorrow," Mary said.

Clara entered the double doors of the library just then. "Are you talking about Joe?" she asked.

"Thank you for calling, William. I must be off now," Mary told him and hung up the phone. She looked guilty as though she had just been caught. "Yes, we were talking about Joe. I asked William to inquire with the hospitals to see if Joe may have turned up in one."

Clara put her hand over her heart. "And did he?"

Mary shook her head. "No one has seen him. William suggested we might ask the police next."

"He'll be here tomorrow for the rehearsal, Mary," Clara said loudly, hands on her hips. "He knows how important this day is. Perhaps he tried to call and couldn't get through because you were on the phone with William."

"We were only trying to help," said Mary.

Clara's voice cracked emotionally as she spoke. "If you really want to help me, you can pick up Joe's suit from the tailor's. They are holding it now but I would rather it be here and ready for him."

"Of course I will pick up the suit, Clara," Mary promised. She then left the library for the grand staircase.

Abigail saw Mary in the upstairs hallway before she

reached her bedroom. "Mary, I have altered your matron of honor dress. Would you like to try it on now?" she asked.

Mary looked at the clock. "Yes, I have a little time, but then I must leave on an errand for Clara."

"All right, Mary. I just want to see how this fits you." They went into the room and Abigail helped Mary into the dress.

"That is much better," Mary said with relief. "I can't feel it pressing me at all. Well done, Abigail."

Abigail smiled. "And how are you feeling? Is your pain any better?"

"I wish I could say yes, but the bruising looks the same as it always has, and the pain is sometimes unbearable. I'm beginning to think I will never feel normal again. I'm considering giving away my old dresses. I don't suppose I'll be able to wear them now that my figure has changed."

"Is that what all these clothes on your bed are for?" Abigail questioned, pointing to the piles of gowns and skirts.

Mary nodded as she hung the matron of honor dress in her wardrobe. "You're welcome to have a look through the clothes to see if there is anything you like."

Abigail began to search through the piles. "But Mary, don't you want to save some of these for when Violet grows up?"

The thought of it made Mary giggle. "It's hard to imagine my little baby ever being old enough to wear these. Won't they be terribly out of fashion by then?"

Abigail laughed. "I suppose they could be, but you might save just a few of your favorites for her."

"Well I did save a special one with Violet in mind," Mary said, reaching to the very end of her wardrobe. "This is the gown I wore for my debutante. I thought Violet might like to try it on when she is sixteen." Mary removed the gown from the garment bag and displayed it for Abigail to see.

Abigail's mouth dropped open and a flood of emotions washed over her. "I don't believe it!"

Mary looked at the gown and then back at Abigail. "What don't you believe?"

Abigail stood up from the bed and went to the dress to run her hand along the sleeves. "I don't know how I never noticed this one in your wardrobe before. I just can't believe it. I—I made this very gown! Or at least, I helped to make the gown—it was so long ago."

Mary was astonished. "How is that possible? Are you certain it was this one?"

"Of course I am certain. I would never forget this dress. So you were the young lady who came into the dressmaker shop that day. I was in the back room when your mother brought you in to be measured," she explained.

Mary groaned at the mention of Mrs. Davenport. "That woman was not my mother. She only pretended to be."

"Yes, I suppose she did," Abigail said quietly. "But Mary, can you believe it? You and I were connected back then—and now we are dear friends and even sisters!"

"It seems an impossible coincidence. But it does make my gown all the more special. Now I look forward to telling Violet the story someday." There was a knock at the door just then. "Come in," Mary said.

Serena Valenti opened the door and walked into the room. "Good evening, Mary. Violet is asleep now," she said.

"Thank you, Serena," Mary told her. "Perhaps she'll sleep through dinner time and you won't have to come back tonight."

"Yes—um—there is something I need to speak with you about," Serena began hesitantly.

"Oh, I will leave you two so you may talk," Abigail said, heading for the door.

"It's alright, Abigail. You can stay for what I have to say. You see, I received an invitation from my parents to return to Pittsburgh. They will allow my daughter and me to live with them."

"Serena, that's wonderful," said Abigail. "I know you've missed your mother terribly."

Serena nodded at Abigail. "I have. To know that I may be part of the family again is my dream come true. The only thing is, I will be in Pittsburgh of course, so I won't be able to help Mary with the baby anymore. I'm sorry, Mary."

"I understand," Mary replied, forcing a smile. "I am happy for you and Angelina."

"I will stay for Clara's wedding of course, but I plan to take the train to Pittsburgh the next day. I hope you'll be able to find someone else to help with Violet."

"I'll begin looking right away. Thank you for telling me, Serena," Mary said.

Serena nodded and said goodnight to the ladies before closing the bedroom door behind her. Mary sat down on the bed. "Oh Abigail, what will I do without her?"

"You must have someone to help you while you heal, Mary. That's all there is to it. We will find a suitable nanny."

"The sooner the better," Mary said as she lay back on the bed.

"Mary, didn't you say there was an errand you needed to run for Clara?"

Mary sat up again. "That's right, I nearly forgot. I promised to retrieve Joe's suit from the tailor."

"Oh good, Joe has come back," Abigail breathed in relief. "I confess, I was beginning to get worried!"

"He hasn't come back yet, Abigail. Clara wants me to get the suit just the same."

"Oh dear," she cringed. "Well, thank goodness the gossip column hasn't caught word about a missing groom. Clara might die if she read about herself in the paper."

"Well don't count out the gossip column yet," Mary said carefully. "There are still three days until the wedding."

Chapter 4

"Clara!" Mary cried frantically as she rushed to Clara's side.

It was early in the morning when Mary found Clara lying slumped over the desk in the library. Clara lifted her head and looked drowsily at Mary. "I must have fallen asleep," she said.

"You frightened me half to death! When Jane said you never retired to your bed last night, and then I found you here…like this…" Mary felt a sinking feeling as she remembered the time she found Mr. Davenport, the father who raised her, slumped over the same desk in the library five years before. Mary shuddered as the memories played out in her mind. She tried to forget them so she could regain her composure. "Did you sleep here all night?" she asked Clara.

Clara sat up straight in the chair. "I suppose I did sleep here all night. I came to the library after dinner so I wouldn't miss any telephone calls. Joe arrived home to his cottage last night and did not want to wake me. I will go see him now."

Mary looked at Clara worriedly. "Clara…did you get into the stored wine this morning?" she asked.

Clara laughed but still seemed drowsy. "Oh Mary, I've not had any of that since it was outlawed. Why do you ask?"

"You don't seem like yourself," Mary answered. "But I am glad that Joe has returned safely. Did you speak to him last night?"

"No," Clara said with a sigh. "I never saw him."

"But he telephoned to say he was coming?" Mary prodded.

Clara shook her head. "He didn't want to wake up everyone in the house with the sound of the telephone."

Mary continued carefully. "Then how did you know that Joe returned last night?"

"Well of course he returned, Mary. Today is the wedding rehearsal. He wouldn't leave me to rehearse all alone," Clara said matter-of-factly.

"Clara dear, I think you must be very tired. Let's get you to bed."

"I can't go to bed now, Mary. There is so much to be done for the wedding. And I want to see Joe, of course."

"All right. Just please wait for me to get ready and I will visit the cottage with you," Mary told her. She winced in pain as she helped Clara stand up from the chair. "On second thought, perhaps Abigail may accompany you. I think I need to lie down." Clara nodded and sat back down in the chair.

Mary held her stomach in pain as she went up the grand staircase. Abigail saw her in the hallway. "Mary, are you all right?" she asked.

"No, I'm not all right," Mary whispered. "I tried to help Clara out of her seat and…I think I hurt myself."

"Here, lie down in my room," Abigail said.

"I will be fine, but Clara needs you," Mary told her. "She is not acting her normal self. I wondered if she found some wine, but she would not admit to it…she wants to see Joe at the cottage and I think someone should go with her."

"I understand. I will go with her," Abigail said, gently covering Mary with her soft quilt. "Be sure to stay in bed so you can rest."

At the stables of Davenport House, Ethan and Sam were releasing the horses into the pasture. "I've got to go down to the ranch now and tend to the livestock," Sam told Ethan.

"Is he still not back yet?" Ethan questioned.

Sam shook his head. "It isn't right what he's doing to Miss Clara…making her wait and not telling her where he is. Miss Clara is too nice a lady. If I were her, I'd call off the whole thing."

Ethan nodded in agreement. "Abigail said she doesn't think Joe is coming back."

"Well I hope Miss Clara gives him a piece of her mind if he ever does come back. She deserves better than the likes of him," Sam said in a huff, then left the stable.

Back at the house, Fiona was showing Mrs. Spencer the plant watering schedule in the conservatory. Through the large glass windows, they could see Clara and Abigail approaching the house from the gardens. Fiona lowered her voice. "Miss Clara went to see if Mr. Joe had returned yet."

"I see," Mrs. Spencer said with a nod. They left the conservatory and opened the back door for Clara and Abigail to walk through. Fiona looked at them expectantly but Abigail discreetly shook her head in answer to Fiona's unspoken question. Clara did not act as though anything were wrong.

"How is the dinner for the rehearsal coming along, Fiona?" she asked.

"Very well, Madam," Fiona answered. "It will be a fine dinner indeed."

"Perfect," Clara said, then she walked past the servants with Abigail following behind. As they went up the grand staircase, Clara told her, "I think I am going to lie down in my room and rest for awhile. It will be a long night and I want to be sure I look refreshed."

"I will tell the others that you are not to be disturbed," Abigail replied. Clara retired to her bedroom for the day and Abigail went to her own room where Mary still lay on the bed.

"Oh good, I hoped you would still be in bed when we returned. How are you?" Abigail asked.

"I will be all right. Was Joe—?" Mary started to ask but Abigail shook her head.

"When we got to the cottage, it was clear he was not there. Clara wants to continue with the rehearsal dinner tonight anyway."

"Oh dear. Should we stop her? Surely Joe would have sent word by now if he was delayed. He can't still be coming, can he?" asked Mary.

Abigail looked at her sadly. "I don't think there will be a wedding, Mary."

Mary looked down at her lap. "I've almost thought about hiding the newspapers from Clara. Word is bound to get out, and that gossip writer is merciless. Clara would never recover after being publicly disgraced, especially with how hard she's worked to rise in society. I am surprised we have not seen an article about Clara already…but it just makes me more nervous by the day."

"I think everyone here is more nervous by the day. The minister will be here tonight for the rehearsal unless Clara calls to cancel—but I don't believe she will," Abigail added in a whisper.

Downstairs in the servants' quarters, Jane was in the kitchen conversing with the cook. "What are we going to do with all this food if there's not going to be a wedding?" she asked. Fiona and Mrs. Spencer walked into the kitchen just in time to hear Jane's question.

"Mrs. Spencer, how would you like to answer Jane? She will be taking orders from you soon enough," Fiona said to her.

Mrs. Spencer nodded and turned to the others in the kitchen. "What happens with all the food will be for the Mistress to decide," she said gently to Jane. "It is not our job to wonder about what happens with the wedding, but only to see that Miss Clara is as happy and comfortable as possible. Now, these trays need to go upstairs to the ballroom. The tables have already been decorated."

Jane took two trays into her hands. "Yes, Mrs. Spencer," she said.

"Nicely done," Fiona said with a smile to the new housekeeper.

Mrs. Malone looked as though she had something to say about what was happening in the house, but she held her peace as she had learned to do over the years. The servants continued to ready the house for the wedding rehearsal and dinner that evening.

When Serena arrived at the house with Gabriella, Fiona led them to the ballroom. "What a glorious room!" Gabriella shouted. "Is this where Miss Clara is getting married?"

Fiona quietly left the room while Serena answered Gabriella. "It's a wonderful room, isn't it?"

"Is it time to eat yet? I smell food," Gabriella said.

"I think we should sit in one of these chairs and stay quiet until we're told to do something," Serena replied.

Upstairs in the house, Abigail knocked on Clara's door. Jane, who was attending Clara that night, opened the door and exited the room. Abigail walked in hesitantly when she saw Clara sitting at her vanity table, still wearing her night-gown. "Clara, the minister is here. Serena and Gabriella are here too."

Clara's lips quivered as she turned to look at Abigail. "They're all downstairs waiting? Everyone?"

It pained her to answer. "Everyone except for the groom."

Clara looked down at her vanity table. "I told Jane not to bother helping me dress tonight. I'm making a fool of myself, aren't I? He's not coming. Everyone knows it."

Abigail pulled up a chair to sit beside her. "I'm terribly sorry, Clara. I don't understand what's happened, but it is he who is the fool. Not you."

"What am I going to do, Abigail?" she asked, covering her face with her hands. "I can't go down there and see everyone."

"And no one could expect you to. Don't worry, dear. I will go downstairs and explain. You needn't see anyone just now. Weddings get canceled all the time, you know." Abigail rose from her chair.

Clara groaned pathetically. "But no one has failed more times at getting married than I have. Mary must be embarrassed to live in the same house as me. I ruin everything."

Abigail leaned over and kissed her on the cheek. "Why

don't you lie down and rest. I will tell the servants that you decided to have dinner in your room."

"I'm not hungry, Abigail."

"Then the tray will be here in case you change your mind," Abigail told her, then left the room and closed the door quietly behind her.

When Abigail entered the ballroom downstairs, everyone looked at her expectantly. "I am sorry to announce that there will be no rehearsal taking place tonight. The wedding has been canceled."

Serena raised her eyebrows in surprise, but when she looked around the room at Mary and the others, she realized that she was the only one caught off guard. Fiona showed the minister to the door apologetically, but he seemed to be understanding.

"I hope Clara will be all right," Serena said to Mary after the minister left. "I am sorry to hear this news."

"I am sorry, too," Mary admitted.

"Should I stay to help with Violet tonight?" Serena questioned.

"William is with her upstairs right now. He is not in the wedding party so he came home to be with her during the rehearsal dinner."

Serena hesitated for a moment. "Mary—um—if the wedding is not going to carry on as planned, then I wonder if I might have tomorrow to prepare for our journey to Pittsburgh. I was going to wait until after the wedding of course, but I am anxious to see my family again. I won't take tomorrow off if it's too much trouble, though."

Mary managed a smile. "You should go, Serena. I know how important it is to you."

"Thank you, Mary. I am truly grateful that you gave me

employment. Lord knows our little family needed it. I hope you find someone to replace me very soon."

"I will pray for your safe travels with Angelina," Mary said, holding back a yawn. "Serena, I'm feeling quite tired now and think I will retire early. Goodnight and have a lovely time with your parents." Mary left the ballroom for the grand staircase.

"I'm sorry about this," Abigail told Serena and Gabriella. "I've just asked the servants to put the dinner into baskets for you to take home."

"That was kind of you, Abigail. Thank you," Serena told her.

"Thank you, Miss Abigail. We haven't had good food in a long time. I'm starved!" Gabriella said honestly.

"Well we can't have you starving now, can we," Abigail replied playfully.

Serena spoke up. "Abigail, before I leave, I want to tell you that I am going to leave for Pittsburgh earlier than I anticipated. I don't know when I'll have the chance to see you again."

Abigail smiled at Serena and hugged her. "You may write to me any time. I want to hear how everything goes."

"I will write," promised Serena. "Goodbye, Abigail."

"Goodbye."

The next day, the house was quiet. The servants took down the wedding decorations. Abigail cared for the babies while also taking charge of the house and instructing the servants. Clara stayed in her room, but peered out periodically throughout the day. She looked out just as the new housekeeper was walking past her door. "Mrs. Spencer?" Clara called after her.

"Yes, Madam?" Mrs. Spencer answered eagerly.

Clara handed her a paper. "You know the townspeople better than the other servants. I would like you to personally see to it that my instructions here are followed to the letter."

Mrs. Spencer read over the list. "I'd be happy to, Madam. Is there anything else I may do for you?"

"Just one thing," Clara answered sadly, her voice breaking with emotion. "I don't want to see anyone today. Except for—well if Joe comes back—I want to see him. But please tell the others that I am not to be disturbed."

"I will set your dinner tray on the console table just outside your door," Mrs. Spencer said.

Clara nodded while she looked at the floor, then she closed her bedroom door. Mrs. Spencer went downstairs with the list from Clara and overheard Abigail speaking to Fiona.

"I will telephone the florist and caterers to explain that everything must be canceled," she way saying.

Mrs. Spencer spoke up. "Beg your pardon, Miss Abigail, but Miss Clara has given me instructions not to cancel the florist and catering services."

"Oh?" Abigail responded in surprise.

"It's all right, I will manage everything myself," Mrs. Spencer assured her.

"Thank you, Mrs. Spencer," Abigail said, beginning to feel relief that her own duties might be lessened.

"Miss Clara also asks—" Mrs. Spencer proceeded, "—that no one visit her room today or disturb her in any way—unless it's Mr. Joe coming back."

"Yes, I see," Abigail answered slowly.

"I'll inform the others," Fiona said, stifling a yawn.

"Why don't you go home now, Fiona. I can take everything from here," Mrs. Spencer offered.

Fiona smiled gratefully and prepared to go home to her cabin. Abigail went upstairs to continue tending to the children, and Mrs. Spencer took care of everything else, just as she said she would.

Later that evening, Mary went downstairs to the library to find a different book to read. She was startled to find Clara sitting in the dark on the floor of the library. "Clara—I didn't realize you were in here. Is there anything I may do for you?"

Clara did not answer. She appeared to be staring at the inside of the iron vault where important documents and valuables were stored. Mary wondered if she should say anything more since it appeared that Clara would rather be alone. Mary quietly chose a book and turned to leave the library. She heard the sound of the vault closing behind her, then Clara's voice speaking. "Oh hello, Mary. I was just checking something."

Mary turned to look at her, but Clara stared straight ahead as if in a daze. She walked past Mary and went up the staircase to her room. Mary went up the staircase herself and hoped that Clara would be all right the next day—the day the wedding had been scheduled to take place.

The next morning, Abigail went to Mary's room to help care for Violet. "Mary, you look exhausted," she remarked. "Didn't you get any sleep last night?"

Mary closed her book and tried to answer, but a yawn escaped instead. "I'm afraid I was never able to fall asleep," she answered, but felt guilty that Abigail was doing all the work while she lay in bed. "I can take her today, Abigail. I must get used to it anyway now that Serena won't be coming back and you're leaving tomorrow."

Abigail held the baby out to Mary. "It's no trouble at

all," Abigail assured her. "Ethan is caring for little Patrick in our room, and I do miss holding a baby this small."

When Mary took Violet from Abigail's arms, she winced in pain. "Oh dear. I fear that I really injured myself yesterday when I helped Clara from her chair."

"Let me see how your healing is progressing. We should make sure that none of the stitches came open."

Mary nodded while Abigail placed the baby back into the cradle. Abigail sighed in disappointment when she checked Mary. "The bruising looks worse today. You must stay in bed and not do anything strenuous. Have you spoken to William yet?"

"No," Mary said timidly. "I know that I should, I just hoped it would be better now that I am resting more. I only wish the pain was not so bad that it kept me up all night."

"I'm going to make you some herbal tea that will help you sleep," Abigail told her. "And don't even think about going downstairs to the dining room today. The maids will bring your meals to you."

"If you insist," Mary acquiesced. After drinking the herbal tea, Mary slept through the afternoon while Abigail cared for the children. As dinnertime neared, Abigail plopped down on her bed from exhaustion. "I'm so glad the little ones are finally asleep," she said to Ethan. "Is this what it's like to have two babies? I don't know how my mother managed it with eleven of us."

Ethan chuckled. "I thought you said you wanted to have at least as many children as your mother."

Abigail crossed her arms over her chest playfully. "Perhaps I've changed my mind." There was a knock at Abigail's door just then. She rose from the bed and opened the door to see Mrs. Spencer. When Abigail saw the newspaper she held in her arm, she grew instantly nervous. "Is everything all right, Mrs. Spencer?"

"I thought you might like to know that Miss Clara was in the newspaper today," she answered.

Abigail felt her heart sink and took the paper from the housekeeper. "Thank you for telling me," she whispered. Mrs. Spencer nodded and left down the hallway. Abigail closed the door and read the paper quickly.

"What's the matter?" asked Ethan.

Abigail's heart raced as she skimmed over the article in the gossip column, but her frown slowly changed to an astounded smile. "Oh—it's nothing like I thought it would be at all. It's actually quite good!" She gave the paper to Ethan to read.

WAS CLARA DAVENPORT BEHIND THE YORKTOWN GIFT BASKETS?

Rumor has it that the anonymous donor behind numerous gifts of meals and flower arrangements was none other than Clara Davenport of Davenport House. Families of servicemen and war widows across the county were surprised by gift baskets of fine foods and flower bouquets delivered straight to their doors yesterday evening. Rather than let anything from her canceled event go to waste, Miss Davenport seems to have made lemons into lemonade for the good of the town.

Ethan raised his eyebrows. "Well, I'll be! Clara will be glad to see this."

"I must show her this minute," Abigail said excitedly. "Oh dear, but she said she does not want to see anyone. Perhaps I can slide the paper under her door so she is not disturbed." Abigail left the room and went to Clara's bedroom door down the hallway. She saw the untouched lunch tray that was set on the console table by the door. Abigail thought about laying the newspaper next to the tray, but noticed that Clara's bedroom door was ajar. From the doorway, Abigail could see the canopy bed neatly made in the center of the room, but Clara was nowhere in sight. Jane approached from the servants' stairs just then and removed the lunch tray from the console table. "Is Clara downstairs?" Abigail asked her.

"Miss Clara hasn't left her room," Jane answered.

"Then you haven't gone in to make her bed?"

"Miss Clara gave strict instructions to be left alone. No one has been in her room or seen her since last night."

"I see. Thank you, Jane," Abigail said, and she watched Jane walk away with the tray. Her heart pounded as she pushed the door the rest of the way open. "Clara?" she called, tiptoeing into the bedroom. She looked through the large windows on the other side of the room and could see that Clara's car was still parked in the driveway. Her gaze then settled upon a white envelope that lay against a pillow on the bed. Abigail had a feeling of dread as she picked up the envelope and read the words on the outside.

Dear Mary,

I pray that you and God will forgive me for the committing the unforgivable.

Clara

Abigail hurried back to Ethan with the envelope. "I

think something terrible is happening," she sputtered. "Clara is not in her room and the servants haven't seen her. She left this addressed to Mary."

Ethan read the words on the envelope and immediately opened it to read the papers inside. He looked at Abigail solemnly. "It's her Last Will and Testament. We need to find her before she does anything." Ethan searched the house for Clara while Abigail went outside to find her brother Sam.

The rainy day was rapidly turning dark and stormy. Sam was busy returning the horses to the stable.

"Sam, have you seen Clara?" Abigail asked him frantically.

"Miss Clara told me she was taking a walk this morning before it started raining," he answered. "She's not back yet?"

"No she hasn't come back and I am worried for her. Which way did she go?"

Sam pointed in the direction of the woods. "Let's take the horses and find her quick. The weather is getting bad real fast." The sound of crackling thunder startled both of them as they saddled the horses.

Ethan came running out to the stable just then. "She's not in the house," he shouted over the sound of the pouring rain.

"Sam said that she went for a walk this morning and never came back," cried Abigail. "She went through the woods."

Ethan quickly saddled a horse for himself. "Sam, go see if you can find her at Joe's house. I'll take the trail through the woods. Abigail, stay with the children. You shouldn't be out here in this storm." He could see how distraught she was when he told her to stay behind. "Don't worry, me and

Sam will find her even if it takes all night." He rode off into the rain while Abigail returned to the house.

Ethan remembered to search at the family cemetery where Clara's mother and father were buried. He found barefoot prints in the mud near the graves that led back into the woods. The thunder roared around him and the rain drenched him down to his boots. He rode to the end of the estate where a barbed wire fence surrounded the perimeter. He was about to turn back, but his gaze caught a piece of material on the fence, flapping in the wind. When Ethan got closer, he realized the material was fabric from Clara's dress. It was stained with blood. Ethan felt sick to his stomach as he looked around him, doing his best to guess where to go next. He went with his instinct and left his horse in a nearby outbuilding so he could climb over the barbed wire. On the other side of the fence was a hill that led down to a rushing river. Something in Ethan's heart told him that Clara would be there. His boots slid in the mud as he made his way down the hill to the bank of the river. It was dark, but he could see a figure sitting on the ground near the water. It was Clara, soaked in rain and mud.

"You shouldn't have come for me. I want to die out here," she said in a low voice.

"You don't know what you're saying," responded Ethan. "Come on. Let's go back to the house."

"I can't go back there. Everyone is better off without me. Let's face it, I never really belonged there...or anywhere..."

"They're worried sick about you. We shouldn't make them worry anymore."

Clara shrugged. "It's too late. Now Mary knows I am capable of the worst thing a person could ever do."

"Mary doesn't know about the envelope," he told her, even though he wasn't sure why it mattered.

Clara looked up at him. "She doesn't?"

"There's blood on your dress," he said, stepping closer to her.

Clara laughed. "I cut my leg on that stupid fence! Can you believe it?"

He looked at her skeptically. "Have you been drinking?"

Clara threw her hands up in the air. "Why does everyone keep asking me that? I'm not a lawbreaker, for goodness' sake. I'm just a disgrace in every other possible way…"

"Let me see how bad the cut is," he said. She looked at him blankly. Ethan leaned down and pulled her dress away from her leg.

Clara laughed again. "Ethan, you're a married man! Oh, I only wish I would have married you before, when I still had the chance. I could have married Phillip too. Why did I have to be so stubborn? I could have married either of you and been perfectly happy."

Ethan looked at the cut on her leg as best he could in the wind and rain. "It's not that bad. We can bandage it up at home." The thunder cracked above them.

"Do you know what the worst part of all this is? I know exactly what happened to Joe. I acted like I didn't know, but I did know."

"What do you mean?" Ethan said, although he was afraid to ask.

"He left me. The day I told him it was past my time to bear children—it's what scared him off. I even wondered if he took my money and ran with it like Lawrence did. But I checked the vault last night and every penny was still there. Every penny. Naturally, it could only mean that Joe couldn't handle the thought of being with a useless woman like me!"

Ethan picked her up off the ground and started to carry her up the hill. She screamed at him, "No! I don't want to go back!" Ethan ignored her cries and carried her to the horse that waited for them on the other side of the fence.

When they got back to the house, Abigail ran out to meet them in the front drive. "Oh, thank goodness you're back!"

Ethan appeared exasperated as he helped Clara down from the horse. Clara seemed to have temporarily snapped out of her madness. "Oh, I can't let anyone see my like this! I'm a mess! Please, don't make me face Mary and the servants this way! I don't want them to know."

"It's all right, Clara," Abigail said gently. "Ethan will take you to the stable apartment and you can get cleaned up there. I will bring a dress for you to change into and we can walk back to the house together."

"Thank you, Abigail. I don't know what I would do without you," Clara said.

"Can you bring some shoes for her, and bandages too?" Ethan asked. "She's barefoot and she's got a cut that needs looking after."

"Right away," Abigail said, and hurried into the house.

Clara turned to Ethan. "You won't tell them where you found me, will you? Please, don't tell Mary how awfully I've behaved. I couldn't bear for her to think ill of me."

"I won't say anything to Mary," he mumbled, hoping it would get Clara to move faster toward the stable.

Abigail brought a dress to the stable apartment for Clara. Ethan quietly took her aside while they waited for Clara to wash up.

"Abigail," he said. "I need to go back to our manor house to tend to the horses tomorrow, but I think you should stay here with Clara. I've known her for a long time and I've never seen her this bad before. Maybe William can help her—she's not in her right mind."

"I know, and I agree with you," Abigail said wearily. "But there is something else—Mary is not well. She hasn't healed from her operation and I thought I should to offer to stay with her until she finds a nanny."

"Is Mary going to be all right?"

"I think so. She needs the chance to rest."

Ethan hugged her close. "You're going to be overworked between looking after her and Clara and the children. I'll take Patrick with me back to Philadelphia."

Abigail smiled gratefully and looked into his eyes. "I will miss my little boy, but you're right that he should go home with you."

"Um—I'm ready," Clara said humbly as she stepped into the room. "Abigail, I'm so sorry for everything I've put you and Ethan through tonight. I'm grateful you came to help. I don't even know how I walked all the way to the river today. When I left the house, I only meant to go to the cemetery and come right back. I don't know what happened to my shoes, either."

"I am glad that you are safe, Clara," Abigail told her. "Now let's get you back to the house."

After Clara had settled into her room for the night, Abigail went to check on Mary, who was just waking up in her bed. "What a wonderful sleep," she said groggily. "Is everything all right, Abigail? You look rather tired yourself. I hope my Violet didn't give you too much trouble."

"She was the perfect angel," Abigail replied.

"Will you still be leaving tomorrow if the weather is like this? The thunder woke me up a few times," Mary said.

"I'm not leaving tomorrow, Mary. I've spoken to Ethan about it and we decided that I will stay here…for you and Clara…until you are both feeling better."

Chapter 5

The next day, Mary went downstairs to the library telephone to call William at the clinic. "Good morning," she said to him. "I'm calling to see if you're all right."

"I'm sorry I didn't come home last night," he said. "I'm afraid that I've lost both of my nurses here."

"Oh dear, what happened?" asked Mary.

"It wasn't just a rumor about the doctor coming to town. The nurses who worked for me had a better offer to work at the new hospital…and I can't possibly pay them as much as what the hospital can. I'm afraid I'll be working late more than usual. But don't worry, I will come by this afternoon to see Clara."

"Why are you coming to see Clara?" asked Mary, unaware of the previous night's events.

"The others say she is not well and hasn't been herself."

"I suppose it can only be expected," reasoned Mary. "She did seem rather in a daze the last time I saw her. I spoke to Clara in the library but she never responded—then a few moments later she seemed surprised to see me there. But is it anything she would require a doctor for?"

"It's hard to say," answered William. "If she has brain fever like I think she might, it has potential to become very serious."

"Brain fever," Mary repeated. "How does it happen?"

"It can be caused by trauma…or in this case, heartbreak. Do you remember the way you became when I told you about the Lusitania sinking? It was years ago."

Mary sighed. "I hardly remember anything that happened during that time."

"I think you had a touch of brain fever. You were unresponsive to the world around you. We were fortunate it only lasted a week—some cases can last for years."

"Poor Clara," said Mary. "How can we help her? Is there a cure?"

"I'm afraid there is no cure. Sometimes it comes and goes, sometimes it sticks with a person. I'm sure you can help Clara by taking charge of the house and ensuring she receives her meals while she recuperates."

"I can do that," Mary said quietly.

"I have to get back to my work, Mary. I'll see you later this afternoon when I come for Clara. Goodbye."

"Goodbye, William." Mary placed the telephone receiver into the cradle and stared in front of her. Fiona walked by the library double doors and saw Mary sitting at the desk.

"Miss Mary?" she said from the doorway.

"Yes, Fiona, what is it?"

Fiona shyly approached her at the desk. "I wanted to tell you that today will be my last day working at the house. Mrs. Spencer seems to have everything under control now. But I wondered if I could come to you with questions I might have, about the baby, when I don't work here anymore."

Mary smiled compassionately. "Of course you can come to me with anything you need."

"Thank you, Miss Mary. We are fortunate to have a midwife living so close by."

"You will be missed very much. Do you think Mrs. Spencer is up to the challenge of filling your shoes?"

"She seems to be adjusting very well. I really believe she cares for Miss Clara and wishes to see her happy," Fiona answered. "In a way, she almost reminds me of Mrs. Price."

"Now that you mention it, I think I see it too," Mary said, rising from her seat. "Abigail must have been right that it was meant to be."

"Miss Mary, there is one other thing I wanted to speak to you about. When Sam was clearing brush from our property, he found an old grave. I was going to tell Miss Clara about it, but did not wish to bother her. I remembered that your family owned this estate before Clara became Mistress, so perhaps you might know about it."

Mary was caught by surprise. "I didn't know anything about a grave on that part of the estate. What does it say?"

Fiona shrugged. "Not much of anything. I couldn't see the dates engraved and the overgrowth made it difficult to make out the name. We won't disturb the grave, of course."

"I wonder if it is the grave of a servant since it was placed so far from the family cemetery. Do you mind if I have a look?"

"I'd be glad to show you," Fiona said. "We can take the horses over since it's a rather long walk to the property."

Mary clutched her stomach anxiously as she thought

of how painful it would feel to ride a horse. "It's all right, Fiona. I'll drive us over in my car."

At the Valentis' farmhouse, Serena was folding up the letter she had just written. "Brother, would you see that this message gets to Clara…when she is not quite so distressed," she said, handing Phillip the letter.

"Sure, I can do that." He put the letter in his pocket and pointed to the carpet bags on Serena's bed. "Are these ready to go?"

"Yes, it's all ready to go to the car. It was kind of Clara to let us drive it to the train station," Serena remarked. "I hope she'll be all right."

While Phillip was loading the luggage into the back of the car, he smelled smoke. His heart pounded furiously when he looked back at the farmhouse and saw smoke rising from a blackened outside wall. He raced through the front door and shouted, "Serena! Get the children out!"

Serena pulled the three children from their bedroom and rushed them outside the back door while Phillip battled with the flames above the cook stove in the kitchen.

"Oh no! I forgot to close the firebox!" cried Gabriella. Serena told the children to wait in Clara's car while she went back into the house to help her brother.

Serena was relieved to see that Phillip had put out the last of the flames. Smoke and soot were everywhere. "Are you all right, brother?"

"Open all the doors and windows," he instructed between coughs. Serena obeyed and soon the smoke in the farmhouse began to thin. Phillip went outside for fresh air while Serena surveyed the damage.

"Did you get the fire out, Papa?" Gabriella asked tearfully.

"The fire's out," he said. "But the kitchen's ruined."

"I'm sorry," she cried. The younger children looked on helplessly.

Serena came out of the house and coughed to clear her lungs. "The bedrooms are all right," she sputtered. "Don't worry, brother. I won't go to Pittsburgh. I'll stay to help with the children while the kitchen is repaired."

Phillip groaned as he watched the remaining smoke pour out of the house. "That's not going to work, Serena."

"Then what can I do to help?" she asked sadly.

"The whole kitchen is a wreck. The children can't stay here while the house is like this. Just take them all to Pittsburgh with you while I get the house figured out."

"You want me to take Gabriella and Donnie with me to our parents' house?" she questioned.

"At least I know that if they are with our mother, she will feed them well—which is more than I can do myself right now."

"I'll go pack a bag for them. There is still time for us to make the train," Serena told him, then headed back into the farmhouse.

Back at Davenport Estate, Mary drove with Fiona to the parcel of land where Sam had build his homestead. Fiona directed Mary where to park the car in order to see the grave. They were surprised to see that Sam and Ethan had just arrived at the same place on horseback. Ethan walked over to the car to open Mary's door for her. "Mary, Sam told me about the grave here and I came to check it out, but I don't think you should look," he warned.

"Why?" she asked, feeling perplexed. "Did you find out who it belonged to?"

Ethan and Sam looked at each other in a strange way. "We don't know," he answered.

"Then why shouldn't I see it?" she asked.

"We were able to clear off the stone so we could see the name," Ethan said solemnly.

"What does it say?" asked Fiona.

Mary walked past Ethan and leaned down to look at the tombstone herself. She gasped when she read the inscription.

Here Lies

MARY LORRAINE DAVENPORT

"It's—it's my name," Mary said with a shudder. "Did you know anything about this grave, Ethan?"

"Pa told me there was a grave somewhere on the estate that had been here for awhile. I never saw it until now."

"I suppose it just means that a relation of mine was buried here," Mary reasoned. "It must be who I was named after. I only wonder why it was placed so far from our family cemetery." She did not want to admit to them that she was still shaken up from seeing her own name.

"We were going to put an orchard on this plot, but we'll be sure not to plant too close," Fiona assured her.

Mary began to feel nauseated. "I think I should get back to the house now," she said weakly. But before she made it back inside the car, her vision went black and she began falling to the ground.

Abigail was by Mary's side when she awoke hours later. "Mary, are you all right?"

She breathed deeply. "I had the strangest dream," she answered. "Is William here yet?"

"He left after seeing Clara this afternoon. It was just before Ethan brought you home. Honestly, Mary, I told you not to even go downstairs, and you ended up on the other end of the estate!" scolded Abigail.

"I did?" Mary asked in confusion. "What happened?"

"Ethan said you fell unconscious while visiting Sam's property," Abigail explained.

Mary cringed. "Oh, then it wasn't a dream."

"You need to be staying in bed," Abigail said, giving her a stern look. "How did you end up at Sam's place?"

"Well I had to go downstairs to call William this morning. Fiona saw me and told me about a grave on their property and I went to see it with her. I promise I won't leave my bed again tonight…just as soon as I get something from the library."

"You are not going downstairs," Abigail said firmly. "Tell me what it is you need from the library and I'll get it for you."

Mary felt guilty for being such a bother. "Will you please bring up the family Bible? I want to check something."

"I will bring up the Bible, but you had better still be in bed when I return," Abigail said.

"I will be," promised Mary. "Oh, did William say what was wrong with Clara?"

Abigail's expression became sad. "He confirmed that it was brain fever. We must look after Clara while she recovers."

Mary hated to think of Clara in such a state. "Poor Clara. I hope she is cured soon."

"We can only hope and pray that she is."

Chapter 6

"Rather than let anything from her canceled event go to waste..." Mrs. Malone read dramatically to the housemaid, "...Miss Davenport seems to have made lemons into lemonade for the good of the town."

Jane's eyes were wide as saucers and she listened to the cook read the article aloud. They were huddled together near the cupboards in the kitchen. "Why, that's nothing like the other stories at all," remarked Jane, who was always keen to hear the town's gossip—even if it was a day old by the time the servants saw the newspaper.

Mrs. Malone folded the paper and hid it between the breadbox and the cupboard. "It's odd isn't it? Now who do you suppose knows so many details about the people in this town, yet won't say an ill word about Miss Clara?"

Jane was bewildered. "I have no idea. Do you?"

Mrs. Malone smiled mischievously. "I've got my suspicions."

"Oh, do tell! Please won't you tell?" begged Jane.

Mrs. Spencer entered the kitchen just then. "What is it you need to know, Jane?" she asked.

Jane looked at Mrs. Malone, but Mrs. Malone shook her head in warning. "Um—I just wanted to know what is on the menu for tonight," Jane lied rather miserably.

Mrs. Spencer raised her eyebrow at Jane. "Shouldn't you be making up the ladies' rooms now?"

Jane looked down at the floor. "Right away, Mrs. Spencer," she said.

After Jane left for the servants' stairs, Mrs. Spencer turned to Mrs. Malone. "Are you going to tell me what that was really about?"

"It was nothing, Ma'am," she answered, slowly wiping the butcher block table with her apron.

"I see," replied Mrs. Spencer, even though she was not convinced. "Then carry on, Mrs. Malone."

Upstairs in the house, Mary checked the Bible for the tenth time to see if a relative of the same name was listed in the Davenport family records. Abigail walked into the room to check on her. "How are you feeling today, Mary?" she asked.

"I'm all right," Mary said distractedly. "Did Ethan tell you about the tombstone we saw yesterday?"

Abigail nodded. "He mentioned it before he left for Philadelphia this morning. It must have been terribly unsettling for you. Have you found any answers to who was buried there?"

"I'm afraid not," Mary said, closing the family Bible and handing it to Abigail. "I was never told that I was named after anyone."

Abigail sat at the tea table and poured a cup for Mary. "How did you sleep last night?"

"Very well, thank you. The tea you are giving me is certainly helping. How is Clara?" asked Mary.

"She keeps to her room. She asks that no one disturb her unless a letter comes from Joe. The only words she speaks to me or the servants are about whether a telephone call or letter has come for her."

"It's a shame," replied Mary. "And no one knows what happened with Joe."

"Sam told me that a man came by the ranch this morning to collect Joe's livestock. He even had a bill of sale signed by Joe himself."

"Then I suppose it means Joe is still alive, at least," Mary said. "It's awful the way he has left Clara like this with no explanation. If I were her, I would not want to hear from him at all!"

"Even so, she seems desperate to receive word from him. I only hope she can recover from this. Oh Mary, I nearly forgot to tell you. Firstly I will tell you that everyone is all right—but there was a fire at the Valentis' farmhouse."

Mary's face fell. "Oh no. Do they need a place to stay?"

"It is only Phillip there now. Last night when he returned Clara's car, he explained that Serena and all of the children went on to his parents' home in Pittsburgh. Phillip is staying behind to repair the damage," Abigail replied.

"I wish there was something we could do to help. Oh Abigail, I feel so useless lying here all day while you and the others do everything. I've decided to see William at the clinic tonight and tell him about the pain."

Abigail was relieved. "I am glad you will finally tell him. At the very least, William can give you medicine to help with the pain."

"I would take it gratefully. Abigail, I'm certain you are anxious to get back to your son. I will try not to take up too much more of your time," Mary said bashfully. "I'm going to write an advertisement in search of a nanny."

"I'm sure you'll find someone soon. Most of all, I hope that you and William find a solution to help you heal," Abigail said kindly.

"Thank you, Abigail. I hope so too."

Later that afternoon at the Valentis' farmhouse, Phillip was busy repairing the kitchen wall. He was startled to hear a knock on the open door. He took a handkerchief from his pocket and wiped his hands and face before answering the door.

"Serena?" called Clara's voice.

Phillip went to meet Clara at the door. "Serena's not here. It's just me."

"Oh—hello Phillip," she said. Her face appeared pale and tired, but a hint of concern was evident through the sadness. "My housekeeper told me about the fire. I came to see if Serena and the children needed new clothes or anything else."

"I should have listened to you about cleaning out the chimney before it was too late," he admitted. "We're lucky the fire was contained to the kitchen. I asked Serena to take all the children with her to our parents' house. At least now I know my children will eat well and I can get the house ready."

Clara nodded but her expression was stoic. "I meant to tell you that Gabriella is welcome to come over to the house and learn how to properly use a cook stove—under the watchful eyes of our cook, of course. I suppose I haven't had the chance to come by and say anything the last few days."

"It's understandable," Phillip replied. Clara looked down at the floor and Phillip decided to change the subject.

"I only wish I had put the house on the market before any-thing like this happened."

She looked up at him. "You are moving?"

"I think so," he said. "I can't find enough work here to make ends meet anymore. I'll have to move the children back to the big city so we can—well, so we can start over. I discovered I'm no good at raising crops. I thought I could learn, but when my family is depending on me, there's not much room for mistakes. I'm no farmer."

Clara seemed deep in thought while Phillip spoke. She responded in a serious voice, "You may not be a farmer, but you are a father and a war hero. You earned your right to be a citizen. At least you have respectable things to your credit."

"Doesn't seem to count for much right now," he grum-bled. Then he cringed. "Forgive me, Clara. I shouldn't com-plain to you of all people. You gave me work and helped our family make it this far. It was ungrateful of me to say those things just now."

"You can be honest with me, Phillip. In fact, I wish everyone would be honest with me instead of only trying to say nice things all the time."

Phillip thought a minute before saying what was on his mind. "If you mean it, Clara, then you won't mind me saying that I knew there was something about that Joe Blake I didn't trust. I'm sorry I didn't say anything before, but I didn't figure it was any of my business."

"Do you know where he is?" Clara asked suddenly.

Phillip shrugged. "I don't know the answer to that. I just know what it seemed like to me."

"And…how did it seem to you?" she prodded.

"It seemed to me that he wasn't forthright about the

reason he moved here—maybe like there was something in his past he was trying to hide."

This was news to Clara. She was under the impression that everyone approved of Joe, yet even though she asked for honesty, she was beginning to feel uncomfortable to hear so much of it at once. "You've given me a lot to think about today," she said. "I am very sorry about the fire. How long will it take to have the kitchen back together?"

Phillip chuckled ironically. "It would go a lot quicker if I had help, but I'll just keep working at it 'til it's done. Maybe a week or two."

Clara noticed that one of his arms appeared to be burned from his elbow down to his hand. "Oh no, you can't work like this," she said, pointing it out.

Phillip looked at his arm momentarily before continuing to remove damaged pieces of the wall. "I suppose I did that when I was getting the fire out. I've worked a lot harder with a lot worse injury, though. It's fine—don't worry about me, Clara. The house will be as good as new soon enough."

"See? I told you I was tired of people saying things just to be nice," she reminded him. "It's clear you're hurting. Why don't you stop the repairs until your arm gets better?"

Phillip stopped what he was doing and stared in front of him. "I suppose it's because even when we're hurting, we have to find a way to keep going."

Clara looked at the blackened wall that was half torn down while the words sunk in. "I should be getting back now," she said quietly. "You know that you can always come to the house if there is anything you need. Our cook will make extra to be sent for you while your kitchen is out of service."

"I appreciate that, Clara," he said humbly. He watched

her turn around to leave. "Wait—I almost forgot." Clara turned to face Phillip while he took a folded note from inside his pocket. "My sister wanted you to have this."

Clara took the note from him and nodded, then turned again to leave through the door. As she walked back to Davenport House, Sam suddenly ran out to meet her.

"Miss Clara," he began, "I'm sorry to bother you, but I just wondered if you heard about Mr. Blake today."

Clara felt her stomach turn into knots while both hope and dread filled her heart. "What did you hear? Has he come home?"

"No Ma'am. I don't think he's coming back. A man came by to take the livestock away. He had a Bill of Sale from Mr. Blake."

Clara's heart pounded in her ears. "Did he say anything about Joe?"

Sam shook his head. "Just that he bought all his livestock two days ago and was here to pick it up."

"Thank you, Sam," Clara said, trying to keep her composure. "I am grateful that you helped with the animals like I asked you to while Joe was away."

"Sure thing, Miss Clara. I'm sorry," he said, hanging his head.

Clara felt tears stinging her eyes as she stumbled back into the house. She went straight to the library and closed the double doors behind her.

Upstairs in the house, Mary was getting ready to leave for Yorktown. She went to Violet's cradle in the bedroom to kiss her goodbye.

"Softly, now," warned Abigail with a smile. "I just got her to sleep."

Mary smiled back at her. "I won't wake her," she whispered. "I just can't stand to be away from her so much."

Abigail held back tears as she thought of her son Patrick being so far in Philadelphia. "Do you want me to come with you to see William?" she asked.

"It's you who should be resting now," Mary said thoughtfully. "I won't be gone long."

"Abigail?" Clara's voice called suddenly from the doorway of the bedroom.

Abigail was surprised to see her. "Good evening, Clara. Is there anything I can do for you?" she asked.

"Ethan is on the telephone," Clara announced quietly.

Abigail exchanged worried glances with Mary, then hurried downstairs to the library. Clara peered past Mary to see Violet sleeping peacefully in the cradle. "You're so fortunate, Mary. You have no idea."

"How are you feeling?" asked Mary. "It's the first time I've seen you since that night in the library."

Clara looked confused. "What night in the library?"

"Well, you were there checking the vault," Mary reminded her. "I was looking for a book and we spoke for a moment."

"I don't remember that, Mary. But I have something important to tell you before I retire to my room for the night. I wanted to tell Abigail too, but she had the telephone call from Ethan."

"It must be the first time Ethan has ever used the telephone—I hope everything is all right," Mary said, seeming distracted. "What did you want to tell me?"

Clara stood up straight. "I've decided to sell the house."

Mary's mouth fell open at the sudden declaration. "You have?"

"Yes, I think it is for the best."

"Clara, I don't mean to be rude, but it seems a bit drastic under the circumstances. Perhaps you shouldn't be making such a decision right now."

"Why not?" Clara asked loudly. "Joe is gone! He sold his livestock and hasn't bothered to tell me anything about his plans! I'm going to be the town spinster, exactly as I've feared. Trust me, Mary. It's best if I can just begin over somewhere else. I need a fresh start."

"All right, Clara," Mary said quietly. "I will tell William tonight and we can discuss other living arrangements."

Clara nodded, then turned on her heel to leave for her bedroom. Mary went downstairs to leave the house but had a bad feeling when she passed the library. Abigail was there, speaking on the telephone and holding her hand over her heart.

"And you'll telephone first thing in the morning if it hasn't gone away?" Abigail questioned, clearly in distress. "All right, then. And you'll tell me if he gets worse? Yes. Goodnight, Ethan." She had tears in her eyes when she looked at Mary. "Patrick has a fever."

"Oh the poor dear," Mary responded. She did not want to alarm Abigail with a stronger reaction since they had both witnessed the terrible epidemic that recently devastated the country.

Abigail sat down on the chair in front of the desk. "I told Ethan to call first thing in the morning if Patrick doesn't improve during the night. I may have to leave earlier than I planned. Forgive me, Mary."

"You need not worry about us," Mary assured her. "I'm going to see William tonight, and Clara is feeling well enough to leave her room at least. You mustn't feel guilty about leaving."

"Did you speak to Clara just now after I left?" Abigail asked, grateful to change the subject.

Mary sighed. "I did. She said that she will sell the house."

"Oh?" Abigail stood up but tried to downplay her shock. "What brought this about?"

"I'm not sure. Apparently she found out about Joe selling off his livestock. I think she's finally given up on him returning."

"Clara is suffering from the brain fever, though. Perhaps she'll change her mind about selling the house before anything goes too far. Poor Mrs. Spencer only just started working here."

Mary nodded and looked at the clock. "I must leave for town now, Abigail. I want to drive over while it is still daylight."

"Of course, Mary," Abigail said, slowly lowering herself into the chair again. She picked up the newspaper from the desk and studied the next day's train schedule.

On Mary's drive to Yorktown, she slowed her car when she came to the old mercantile that William told her would be the new hospital. A sign had already been placed at the top of the building: YORKTOWN HOSPITAL with a smaller sign that read: OPENING SOON.

Mary parked her car and walked up to the entrance. She noticed a sign in the window with a portrait of a woman accompanied by words that made Mary gasp and laugh at the same time:

```
Painless Childbirth!
Yorktown Hospital offers
Twilight Sleep!
```

"If only there were such a thing as painless childbirth," she marveled aloud. She looked in the windows and could see that hospital beds and other furniture had already been put into place in the new hospital. Mary returned to her car and drove the rest of the way to William's clinic.

The little bell above the door sounded when Mary walked into the clinic. "I'll be with you in just a moment," William's voice called from behind a curtain. Mary sat down in the waiting area until the patient with William emerged from behind the curtain and left through the front door. "Mary!" William said in delight when he pulled open the curtain. "What a lovely surprise."

Mary smiled and realized it had been too long since she heard his voice. She rose from her seat. "I missed you," she said honestly.

"I've missed you too," he said. He lay down on one of the clean beds and groaned in exhaustion. "I'm so tired, Mary. Just pray that no one else comes through the doors tonight. I'm not sure I can stay awake another minute!"

"Oh," Mary said quietly. She watched him close his eyes and start to breathe deeply. "I can come back another time."

"Please stay and talk to me," he murmured, still closing his eyes. "I want to hear your voice. How are things at the house?"

"Where do I begin? Clara told me she intends to sell the house," Mary replied.

"That seems drastic. Perhaps she'll change her mind tomorrow. You can't trust everything she says right now."

"She seemed rather serious," remarked Mary. "What will we do if she does sell the house?"

William opened his eyes and turned his head to face her. "In all seriousness, we may need to move anyway. If I can't staff the clinic to treat as many patients as we used to, I don't know how we'll keep the doors open. I even wrote to ask the board of directors of the new hospital to see if I could get a position with them. They answered that they have enough doctors coming in and won't need my services. I wanted to tell you all of this sooner…I just never had the chance." He closed his eyes again.

Mary thought about the new hospital building and remembered the sign in the window. "William," she began uncertainly. "Is there such a thing as painless childbirth?"

He chuckled. "I'm afraid that was never the way the good Lord intended it. You've attended enough births by now to know it's not the case."

"Then what is Twilight Sleep?" she asked.

William opened his eyes again. "Where did you see that?"

"At the new hospital. There is a sign in the window that advertises it," answered Mary.

William sat up on the bed, his expression changing from tired to disappointed. "Twilight sleep was developed in Germany. I'm familiar with the method, but I don't like it, Mary. It requires a laboring woman to be injected with morphine and scopolamine—a very strong combination— as a painkiller."

Mary suddenly felt herself getting indignant. "Do you mean that it's true a woman needn't feel the pain? William, how could you not tell me? I nearly died of the pain when I was in labor with Violet!"

"I'm sorry, Mary. I don't think it's safe. The pain for a woman in labor is only temporary anyway."

Mary crossed her arms over her chest. "It must be safe if the new hospital is using it. William, you just can't imagine the pain unless you've been through it yourself. If you had, you would have been eager to help me and the other women in town all this while!" Tears began rolling down her face. "I am going back home now," she said.

"Wait, I don't understand why you're upset like this," William said, pleading at her with his tired eyes.

"That's just it—you don't understand!" she snapped. She stormed away from the clinic and held her sore stomach as she climbed into her car. Mary drove a short way before she parked again and laid her head against the steering wheel. She cried and cried as the months of pain since the day of her operation took their emotional toll.

Chapter 7

The next morning, Abigail and Mary went to the dining room for breakfast. Mary's face felt swollen from her tears the night before. She felt guilty for storming out of the clinic as she had, and she planned to apologize to William later in the day when the clinic would not be busy. Abigail stared blankly ahead of her as if she were in another world.

Mary noticed that Abigail was quieter than usual and had not touched her breakfast. "Is everything all right?" she asked.

Abigail snapped back to reality. "Oh, I'm sorry. I was just thinking about Patrick."

"Have you heard from Ethan this morning?" Mary asked carefully.

"I did," she replied. "He said the fever broke in the night and that Patrick seemed well, but…"

"You must go to him, Abigail. You won't have a moment's peace until you do. If I knew Violet was ill, and I could not be with her, it would drive me mad."

"Thank you for understanding, Mary. How did your visit with William go last night?"

Mary was unsure how to answer without worrying Abigail, since she had not told William about her pain as she promised. "We talked and—I am going to see him again tonight."

"Wonderful, Mary," replied Abigail.

Mrs. Spencer entered the room just then with the morning paper. She placed it on the breakfast table near Mary's plate. "The Yorktown Times, Madam," she seemed proud to announce.

"Thank you, Mrs. Spencer," Mary said. She gasped as she looked it over. "Oh my! Oh, you won't believe this headline, Abigail! Clara will be so pleased!"

She turned the front page to face Abigail:

```
WOMEN'S SUFFRAGE WINS!

FEDERAL AMENDMENT RATIFIED, ENTIRE
NATION OF WOMEN WILL HAVE THE VOTE
               THIS FALL
```

Abigail rose from her seat and clasped her hands together in delight. "What wonderful news! We must show Clara right away!"

The ladies excitedly left the dining room and went up the grand staircase to Clara's bedroom. Abigail knocked on the door. "Clara dear, there is something you must see," she called through it.

Clara opened the door quickly. Her hair was a mess and

she still wore the clothes she had on the previous night. "Is it from Joe?" she asked frantically.

"Um—no it isn't from Joe," Abigail said apologetically. Clara's face fell. Abigail held the paper in front of Clara. "But look at this morning's headline!"

Clara gazed at the paper and read the words over and over until they began making sense in her mind. "Oh," she said quietly. "I suppose it was bound to happen at one time or another." She went to her bed to lie down.

Mary and Abigail exchanged confused glances. "Clara," Mary said gently while approaching the bed. "Did you see the news about the vote? All of your efforts have finally paid off. We may all vote in the election now, just as you have dreamed of!"

Clara shrugged and looked into the distance. "What does any of that matter anymore? Please let me alone so I may sleep—unless a letter comes for me in the post, of course." She closed her eyes.

Mary and Abigail left the room and closed the door behind them. "I hoped she would be happier than that," Abigail said with a frown. "She seems intent on hearing from Joe…but Mary, what if she is waiting a lifetime?"

Mrs. Spencer emerged from the top of the servants' stairs just then and approached the ladies on the landing. She held a silver tray with a thick envelope set on top of it.

"Is that—?" Abigail began to ask.

"A letter for Miss Clara," Mrs. Spencer answered, "delivered by messenger boy." She walked past them to Clara's bedroom and knocked. The ladies watched as Clara took the letter from the tray and immediately closed her bedroom door. Mrs. Spencer smiled as she walked past the ladies back to the servants' staircase.

"I hope that Clara finally gets the answers she was waiting for," Mary remarked.

"I am suddenly hungry again," Abigail said. "Let us go finish our breakfast—if the servants haven't cleared it away yet." They both returned down the grand staircase to the dining room.

"I am worried for Clara, but I also think I should be home with my family," Abigail said quietly. "I could not sleep last night. I ended up packing my suitcase in the event Patrick worsened through the night. There is a train that leaves for Philadelphia in two hours."

"Then I will drive you to the train station myself," Mary said decidedly. "Jane can look after Violet while we are away, and I have to go to town anyway to submit my advertisement for a nanny. I could not sleep last night either—but I did write the advertisement."

"If you cannot find anyone in Yorktown, I might send one of my sisters to come work for you," Abigail said.

Mary smiled. "Thank you, Abigail. We may just have to arrange for that to happen."

Downstairs in the servants' quarters, Jane was in the kitchen with Mrs. Malone. She had been wanting to ask about the cook's suspicions regarding the gossip column, but Mrs. Malone was careful not to say anything while the new housekeeper was about. Mrs. Malone read aloud the previous day's article while Jane listened with interest, although Jane felt as though she might burst from the suspense. "Who do you think wrote it?" she questioned.

Mrs. Malone looked around the kitchen before she attempted to answer. Mrs. Spencer walked in just then to view the chalkboard where the day's menu was written. Mrs. Malone looked Jane in the eye and titled her head toward the new housekeeper. Jane's eyes nearly bugged out of her face. She mouthed the words to Mrs. Malone so she would not be heard out loud, "Mrs. Spencer is the journalist?"

Mrs. Malone nodded with a knowing smile and continued her work chopping vegetables for the soup. Mrs. Spencer suspected that something was going on behind her and turned around to face the cook and housemaid. Jane quickly removed the mop from the wall and moved it across the floor.

"Jane, don't you need a bucket of water for that to be effective?" Mrs. Spencer questioned.

Jane did not look her in the eye while she leaned the mop back against the wall. "Yes, Mrs. Spencer. I'll fetch the bucket right away."

In the city of Yorktown, Mary was driving away from the train station where she had just taken Abigail. She was on her way to the newspaper office and parked her car on the side of the street while she read her advertisement a final time.

"Mrs. Hamilton!" a man's voice called from behind her. Mary turned to see Mr. Walker, the owner and manager of the Yorktown Inn. "Mrs. Hamilton, thank goodness you're here!"

Mary climbed out of the car. "What is it, Mr. Walker? Is everything all right?"

"I'm afraid not, Mrs. Hamilton. There's a lady giving birth in my hotel. My wife is with her right now, but we could really use your help."

"Of course, Mr. Walker. I will come upstairs with you," she answered. Mr. Walker led her up the steps to the hotel and through the lobby to the hallway of rooms. When he opened the door to the correct room, Mary could hear a woman's labored breathing while Mr. Walker's wife conversed with her.

"Now don't waste your time with either of the Hamiltons," Mrs. Walker was saying. "You'll want to see that new doctor that offers painless childbirth. My friend Marjorie had it in Philadelphia and never felt a thing!"

Mr. Walker cleared his throat to announce he had arrived with Mary. "Here she is," he said with a nervous laugh.

"Oh—Mrs. Hamilton—thank you for coming up," stammered Mrs. Walker. "I don't think she's quite that far along though. Ruth, this is Mrs. Hamilton, a local midwife. She can answer any questions you have. I'll just leave you two to talk."

"Thank you, Mrs. Walker," Ruth said, trying to catch her breath. Mr. and Mrs. Walker left them alone in the hotel room.

"Good afternoon," Mary greeted. "How long ago did the pains start?"

"It's been this way for about an hour or so," Ruth answered timidly. "But I think it's too soon to have the baby."

"It could be false labor," Mary said. "Why don't you tell me exactly what you're feeling."

"I feel it tightening just here…but it's not as bad as when I gave birth to my first son," she explained.

Mary watched her carefully and held her hand. "I believe it is only false labor this time. Will you be traveling much longer?"

"Oh, I'm just passing through your town here with my husband. We never meant to stay long, but I started feeling ill and we came here to rest. When my husband left to get us something to eat—that's when the pains started."

"I will stay with you until your husband returns, if you'd like," offered Mary.

"Oh no, that's all right, Mrs. Hamilton. I can't feel it happening anymore now, and I don't want to take up more of your time. Thank you for the help."

"It was my pleasure," Mary said, then turned to leave the room. "I will ask for a pitcher of water to be brought up for you. You must stay well hydrated for your journey."

"Thank you again, Mrs. Hamilton," Ruth said as Mary went to exit the room.

"Oh, pardon me," Mary said to a man who was about to enter the room when she opened the door. She felt her heart stop when she recognized the man who stood before her with an armful of bread and cheese. It was Joe Blake.

"Uh—M—Mary," he sputtered. "What are you doing here?"

"Are you honestly going to ask me what I'm doing here? What are you doing here?" she demanded. "Don't tell me you are the husband that Ruth said she was waiting for."

Joe looked at the floor. "It's a long story," he said.

Mary's mouth dropped open. "Joe, what have you done?"

"First of all," he said defensively, "that's another man's child that Ruth's carrying right now, so don't be telling Clara any different."

"You're hardly in a position to be telling me what I should say to Clara. I assume you explained your long story in your letter to her today?"

Joe shook his head. "I never sent a letter. I know I should have, but…it's not that simple."

Mary tapped her foot on the floor impatiently. "How long have you been married?" she asked.

"It's only happened just this week," he said in a low voice. "I never planned it, and I certainly never meant to hurt Clara."

"Then you have failed," Mary said bitterly. "How could you promise to marry her, and then run off to marry another woman?"

"She's not just another woman," Joe said. "Ruth and I were sweethearts from years ago. She wrote to me the week before I was supposed to marry Clara and said she was in trouble, and that I should meet her in Harrisburg. I didn't know she'd be bringing…our son…to the meeting. I never even knew I had a son. He's four years old, you see. He's with Ruth's mother just now."

"Does Clara know anything about you and Ruth?" Mary questioned.

"No. I never told her," he replied. "When I saw my son for the first time in Harrisburg, I knew I needed to stay with Ruth and be a father. The trouble she got into—well there isn't going to be a father for the child she's carrying now. I only wanted to do the right thing."

"And abandoning Clara without a word that you would miss the wedding was the right thing?"

"I'm real sorry about that," he told her sadly. "Are you going to explain to her?"

Mary was overwhelmed with the new information and unsure how to respond. "Seeing as how it would only devastate her further to know you left her for another woman, I don't see how I possibly can. Why did you come back to Yorktown, anyway?"

"I had to take care of some business," he answered

vaguely. "I never meant to stay more than an hour or two, but Ruth—well she didn't feel too good on the ride over."

"Then I suggest you finish your business in town and never come back," Mary said emotionally. "Let Clara forget about you so she can move on with her life." Mary turned and began walking down the hallway to get away from him as quickly as possible. She began to wish that she had never gone into town that day.

Back at Davenport House, Mrs. Spencer was bringing Clara a tray of tea. To her surprise, Clara opened her bedroom door and spoke to her from the doorway. "Mrs. Spencer," she began. "I believe I may trust you to be discreet with what I am about to tell you."

"Of course, Madam," answered Mrs. Spencer. "You may tell me anything."

Clara gave her a single folded paper. "I need you to complete these things on the list exactly, just as you did with my instructions for the wedding flowers and food."

Mrs. Spencer set the tea tray on the console table and took the list from Clara. "As you wish, Madam."

"There is one more thing," Clara said. She pulled an envelope from her pocket and lowered her voice. "I need you to take this letter directly to the post office. Do not send it with one of the servants or anyone else—it's very important that no one in the house sees this envelope. Do you understand that no one must see or even know about it?"

Mrs. Spencer's eyes grew wide when she read the name the envelope was addressed to. "I understand, Miss Clara," she whispered hoarsely. "I will take it to the post office myself and not another soul shall know of it."

"Very good," Clara said, then closed the door. Mrs. Spencer hurried down the hallway to the servants' stairs.

She did not notice Jane, who was standing just around the corner—and had heard every word of the conversation.

A little while later, Jane strutted into the kitchen and looked smugly at Mrs. Malone.

"You seem awfully proud of yourself," Mrs. Malone commented as she removed a tray of muffins from the oven.

"I *am* proud of myself. For once, I am the one who knows a secret about this house!" Jane closed her eyes and leaned her head back to bask in the glory.

Mrs. Malone laughed. "Oh, out with it already, Jane. I have to get these salads made."

"You were wrong about Mrs. Spencer being the writer of that gossip column," Jane said sensationally.

Mrs. Malone raised her eyebrow. "And how would you know?"

"Because I discovered who the mystery writer is—and it's none other than Miss Clara, herself!"

Mrs. Malone held her belly and laughed. "I don't know for sure who the mystery writer is, but I know for sure it ain't our Mistress!"

Jane was indignant. "It's a better guess that our new housekeeper!"

Mrs. Malone continued to laugh and Jane left sulking from the kitchen.

The next morning at Davenport House, Jane informed Mary that she had a telephone call in the library. Mary thought it must be William, but was surprised to hear Abigail's voice on the other end.

"I am calling to say that Patrick is doing well," Abigail said cheerfully.

"Oh, thank goodness," replied Mary. "Do you think it was just a cold?"

"Looks that way," said Abigail. She then went quiet for a minute and Mary wondered whether she should say anything about seeing Joe the previous day. Abigail was the first to speak. "Mary, I wonder if you could do me a favor."

"Anything," said Mary with a laugh. "After all that you've done for me lately, I may be forever in your debt. What do you need?"

"Would you please go next door and tell Phillip that all is well—with Patrick?"

Mary felt perplexed. "You wish me to tell Phillip Valenti?"

"Yes, please," she confirmed. "I told him about Patrick being ill before I left for the train station yesterday. I just want him to know there is no reason to worry."

"All right," Mary said slowly.

"He is Patrick's godfather, after all," she added.

"Yes, of course," Mary responded. "I will go next door just as soon as I hang up the phone with you."

"Thank you, Mary," Abigail said gratefully. "Have a lovely day."

Mary went upstairs to her room to get ready for her visit with Phillip Valenti. She changed her clothes and checked on her sleeping baby before she returned downstairs. As Mary descended the grand staircase, she could see the new housekeeper pacing anxiously and wringing her hands by the front door. "What is it, Mrs. Spencer?" Mary asked her.

"Um—there's a lady here to see Miss Clara…"

Mary sighed. "Clara is not able to receive visitors."

"That's just it, Mrs. Hamilton. I told the lady that my Mistress was indisposed, but she would not take no for an answer. She kept asking questions about why Miss Clara would not see her."

"Don't worry, I will speak to the lady myself since I'm going outside anyway. I only hope it's not the journalist for that horrid gossip column." Mary wrapped her shawl around her shoulders and walked out the front door. "Good afternoon," she greeted the woman who waited at the bottom of the steps.

The woman had gray hair pulled back into a bun and she stooped forward to balance on a thick wooden cane. Mary was perplexed at the way the woman seemed to stare at her. Mary pulled her shawl tighter around her shoulders as goosebumps covered her arms. She felt relieved when the woman finally stated her business. "I am here to see Clara."

"I am sorry, but Clara is indisposed today," answered Mary. "Would you like me to take a message to her?"

"What's wrong with her?" asked the woman quickly. "She's not ill, is she?"

Mary was taken aback that the strange woman would speak so boldly, but Mary was not about to give her any details. "Again, I am sorry, but as I say she cannot receive visitors just now. I am glad to relay any message you may have for her."

"No bother," the woman muttered. "I need to speak with her in person."

Mary nodded and tried to smile but felt increasingly awkward under the woman's intent stare. "Very well, Ma'am. If you'll just give me your name—I will tell Clara that you stopped by the house to see her."

The woman gaped at her. Mary felt more uncomfortable by the second and regretted that she had not just said goodbye and returned into the house. The woman's voice cracked as she responded emotionally. "Mary! Do you mean to say you don't recognize me? I am your mother!"

Chapter 8

The next morning, Mrs. Spencer walked into the dining room just as Mary was finishing her breakfast. "Miss Clara asks for you to meet her in the upstairs sitting room," she said with a smile.

Mary went up the grand staircase, but paused as she reached the landing. She could hear the sound of laughter coming from the sitting room. It was Clara. Mary realized it was the first time she heard Clara laugh in delight since long before the wedding was to take place. Mary entered the room with Mrs. Spencer following not far behind. Clara was seated in front of the fireplace. "Good morning, Clara," Mary greeted her. "You are looking well."

"Thank you, Mary," Clara replied. "Mrs. Spencer and Jane were just introducing Jimmy, the newest member of our household staff."

Mary stared in surprise at the young boy who stood beside Jane. He looked to be about twelve years old. "Oh—hello, Jimmy," she greeted.

"How do you do, Mrs. Hamilton?" he said politely.

"I am very well," Mary said with a giggle.

"Now Jane will take you downstairs and you will have a tour of the whole house," Clara said to Jimmy. The housemaid left with the boy and Mrs. Spencer laid out tea for Mary and Clara.

"Will there be anything else, Miss Clara?" she asked.

"No thank you, Mrs. Spencer," Clara answered.

After Mrs. Spencer left, Mary turned to Clara. "I am glad to see you feeling better," she said quietly. She decided it was not the time to mention the visit from Mrs. Davenport the previous day. Mary had broken into a run to the Valentis' land the instant she recognized the mother who raised her. But Mary did have something else on her mind to say to Clara. "I'm a little confused about why you have hired a new servant," she began.

"Oh I know that poor Jane has been overworked and waiting for a new maid, so I told Mrs. Spencer we must have more help," she answered plainly.

"But—aren't you planning to sell the house? Where will the servants go when we move?"

"Oh that," Clara said with a laugh. "I changed my mind about selling the house, Mary. I was not thinking clearly when I said those things. I suppose the idea of starting over someplace new has lost its appeal for now. This house is all I've ever known and I'm quite comfortable staying here until the end of my days."

Mary breathed in relief. "I am glad you won't sell the house, but I should tell you that I've already spoken to William and we've discussed relocating to Philadelphia."

"You want to leave?" Clara asked, suddenly appearing as though she might cry.

"It's not that we want to leave, Clara. William applied for a position at the new hospital, but the board of directors declined him. With the majority of the town's business going to a well-staffed hospital, we may need to close the clinic for good."

Clara looked down at her lap. "I see," she replied sorrowfully. "I hope you don't have to go, Mary."

The two ladies sat in front of the fireplace without saying much else. Mary shuddered to relive the previous day's encounter with Mrs. Davenport. She looked at Clara, who seemed like she might be cheered by the excuse to talk about someone else. "You'll never believe who stopped by the house yesterday," said Mary.

Clara covered her heart with her hand. "It wasn't Joe, was it?" she asked, a faint spark of hope still evident in her eyes.

Mary took a deep breath before she announced the news. "No, it was not Joe…it was Mrs. Davenport."

"Oh," Clara responded. "What did she say?"

Mary was taken aback by Clara's casual reaction. "I expected you to be a little more surprised that she came here. I'm still shaking from the meeting, myself!" she exclaimed. Clara continued to look at her expectantly. Mary felt she had no choice but to answer her question. "She did not say what she came for. She only said that she must speak with you in person."

"How curious," Clara said distractedly. When she turned toward Mary again, she looked as if she were experiencing a tinge of guilt. "Forgive me, Mary. I hadn't meant for you to find out this way."

Mary had a sinking feeling. "Find out what? Clara, what are you saying?"

Clara stared at the fireplace again. "I've been corresponding with your mother. She is helping me with some things."

Mary was appalled. "You can't be serious!"

"I am serious, Mary. It was she who convinced me that selling the house would be a mistake."

"Well I suppose I agree with that—but Clara—think of all the terrible things she did to you! And to your mother!"

"I know," she said quietly. "It's in the past now. I only want to move forward at this time."

Mary stood up from the settee. "I can't believe this! I can't believe you would speak to her in the first place, let alone have her come to the house without warning me first!"

"I didn't know she would come to the house. I'm sorry. I was afraid that if I told you about our correspondence, you wouldn't understand…or maybe even be disappointed in me."

"Of course I don't understand!" Mary cried, beginning to shake with anger. "Have you forgotten the way she treated us, and how she deceived you in order to take the estate?"

"I don't believe she would do such a thing to either of us again. She wrote me a letter, Mary. While I was lost in darkness and despair and waiting to hear from Joe, it was your mother who wrote to me. She made me see things in a different light. Let me get the letter from my room so I can show you. There is more to the story than you realize."

Mary began to feel ill to with every word that Clara spoke. She could no longer contain her indignation. "I'm sure she is back to her same old tricks now—now that you have invited her in! And would you kindly refrain from referring to that woman as my mother! She deceived everyone in the house to think I was her daughter, only to deny it all when it became profitable for her. She stole me from my own parents to hide her lies!"

Clara looked at Mary with pleading eyes. "Mary, if you could just see the letter, you might—"

"I won't see it, Clara," she said firmly. "That woman belongs in jail, and nothing you can say or do will convince me otherwise. Did she tell you in her letter about how she poisoned your father?"

Clara looked down at her lap and tears began to fall. "No. She said no such thing."

"I'm sure she only told you what she thought you wanted to hear. Clara, you must cease corresponding with her immediately, for all of our sake's!"

"I'm sorry, Mary. That won't be possible," Clara answered. "You may not understand now, but you will in time."

Mary stood up angrily. "Very well, Clara. Invite her back to the house if you wish, but I will not be here the next time she comes. I'm going to gather mine and Violet's things and be out of your house once and for all—it is bound to be the end result anyway, now that you have chosen to listen to—her!"

"Mary, please don't go," Clara whimpered.

"I have to," Mary said as she exited the room. She added sharply, "And we both know your own mother would be on my side if she were still here." Mary did as she said and packed her things to leave the house with Violet. Clara returned to her room and cried on her bed until she had no tears left to cry.

When Mary arrived at the clinic in Yorktown, she explained everything to William about what had happened with Mrs. Davenport and Clara. William listened quietly as they lay on the small bed in the apartment above the clinic.

Mary let out an exasperated breath after she finished relaying her story. She looked curiously at William when she realized how quiet he had been all the while. "You have not said a word," she said nervously. "Won't you tell me what you think about the way Clara has betrayed us?"

William spoke in a solemn voice. "I think that Clara is in a fragile state of mind right now. Don't forget that she has been afflicted with brain fever. Now is not the time for arguments, but the time to make amends."

Mary frowned and looked down at her quilt. She had been secretly worried that William might respond that way. "Then you don't think I am justified in my anger?"

"I didn't say that. Mrs. Davenport threatened me and my practice too. I can only imagine what she is capable of."

"Yes, exactly!" Mary replied, feeling validated. "Clara thinks that she has changed, but surely the only thing that has changed about Mrs. Davenport is the way she looks. I barely recognized her after just five years! She walks with a cane now...perhaps her weakened appearance is why Clara is no longer afraid. But isn't it our duty to convince Clara that she will ruin everything if she continues on this course?"

"I meant what I said about making amends, Mary. Clara looks to you for approval, much like she looked to her mother for approval while she was alive. She might take it very hard and even harm herself if she thinks you are disappointed in her."

Mary looked at him in confusion. "What do you mean 'harm herself'?"

"I mean the brain fever. I've seen these things take a turn for the worse—even to the point of death—when the person who is suffering feels they have nothing left to lose."

Mary felt her stomach turning. "I didn't realize...I suppose I should not have been so harsh with her. Clara was looking so well today that I never remembered she was ill in the first place." She looked apologetically at William.

"I should not have been so harsh with you the other night, either. I'm sorry. I've been so tired lately, and now that Serena and Abigail have gone, I have no one to help with Violet. I only hope my advertisement for a nanny is responded to soon."

William groaned. "Mary, I am out of money," he confessed. "I don't know how we will pay for a nanny right now. It is only by Clara's good graces that we even have a place to live."

Mary swallowed the lump in her throat. "Then I will cash in my stocks to pay the nanny. I can't do everything on my own with the baby."

"Of course you can, Mary," he replied confidently. "You're stronger than you realize. You need to believe that you are capable, instead of always relying on others for help. We grew up in different worlds, you see. You have spent your life depending on servants but most mothers do not have nannies and they do just fine."

"You don't think I should have the help?" Mary questioned.

William gazed at her endearingly. "I am only saying that you can manage on your own even though you may not know it yet. I'm afraid that I cannot give you the life you've been accustomed to with servants, especially now that I may be out of work. I'm sorry, Mary. But I believe you are perfectly capable. You should withdraw the advertisement."

Mary could not look him in the eye. She turned over in the bed and faced the wall instead of her husband. She suddenly felt unworthy of her privileged life and that she and William might be worlds apart in a way he would never understand. "I will withdraw the advertisement," Mary said as her tears fell silently onto the pillow, "and I will move back into the house with Violet and make sure Clara is all right."

Chapter 9

The next morning at Davenport House, Mrs. Spencer informed Clara that she had a visitor. "Send her into the drawing room," Clara said, taking a deep breath. "I will be down to see her in a moment."

Mrs. Davenport waited on the sofa and looked around the room to see how things had changed since she was Mistress of the house. "Hello Clara," she said when Clara appeared in the doorway.

Clara clenched her fists at her side. "Did you really poison my father? Answer me instantly before I turn you out of this house for good!"

As Clara met with Mrs. Davenport in the drawing room, Mary entered the house with Violet. Mrs. Spencer greeted her at the front door. "Good morning, Mrs. Hamilton. May I help with the baby?" She held out her arms to take Violet.

"Thank you, Mrs. Spencer," Mary said. "I have luggage in my car as well."

"I will send Jimmy to retrieve it right away, Madam," she responded with a nod.

Mary had forgotten that Jimmy worked at the house. She showed him the luggage in the car and explained which room was hers. "I'll get those to your room right away, Ma'am," he responded cheerfully.

The telephone rang just as Mary walked by the library. She sat at the desk and answered the call.

"Good morning, Mary. I called earlier but Mrs. Spencer said you stayed in town last night," said Abigail's voice. "Is everything all right?"

"I don't know that I would call everything all right, but I'm trying to make peace with it," answered Mary. She explained about her argument with Clara the previous day. Abigail remained quiet the whole time. "William's response was that I should make amends with Clara and be considerate of the brain fever."

"I think he is right," Abigail said.

Mary huffed in frustration. "Then I suppose you think I have no reason to be upset that Clara is trusting Mrs. Davenport, of all people. I still don't know how I will face Clara right now."

"I understand that you're upset, Mary, but you must think of Clara. You don't know how bad it got with her."

"What do you mean?"

Abigail sighed into the phone. "Go to the bookcase and look underneath the medical encyclopedia. There's something you should see."

Mary placed the telephone on the desk and went to the bookcase. Under the encyclopedia was an envelope. Mary returned to the desk with the envelope and read the words written on the outside:

Dear Mary,

I pray that you and God will forgive me for the committing the unforgivable.

Clara

"I don't understand," Mary said quietly into the phone. "Why was this hidden from me?"

"You were sleeping the day that Clara left it in her room. It was an emergency, Mary. Ethan and I had to open it so we could act quickly before it was too late. I think it's time for you to see what Clara wrote inside."

Mary removed the papers from the envelope. She swallowed painfully when she saw that it was Clara's Last Will and Testament.

I devise, bequeath, and give my wardrobe to my friend and neighbor, Serena Valenti.

I devise, bequeath, and give my jewelry to my friend, Abigail Smith.

I devise, bequeath, and give Davenport House, and all the rest and remainder of my estate, to my beloved friend, Mary Hamilton.

Tears welled in Mary's eyes as she read the page. "Oh Abigail, I'm afraid to know what Clara was thinking when she left this in her room that day." She paused and took a deep breath. "I will be gentle with her."

Jimmy appeared in the doorway just then and stood outside the library while Mary ended her call with Abigail. "What is it, Jimmy?" she called to him.

"Mrs. Spencer said I should ask if you needed anything else, Ma'am," he said, appearing to be suddenly nervous.

Mary smiled at him. "I would grateful if you could take some books to my room. They are rather large and heavy. I will show you which ones."

Jimmy hesitated outside the doorway. "I'm afraid I can't go in there, Ma'am," he said.

"It will be all right," Mary said. "I'll explain to Mrs. Spencer that I asked you to."

Jimmy looked at the floor. "I can't go in because I'm scared."

Mary rose from her seat and walked to be closer to Jimmy by the door. "What is there to be scared of?" she asked, motioning around the room. "There are just books."

"A man died in there…right where you were sitting at the desk, Ma'am," he replied.

Mary suddenly felt goosebumps cover her arms and her heartbeat quickened. She attempted to compose herself. "Did one of the maids tell you that?" she asked.

Jimmy shook his head.

"Jimmy, come down to the kitchen to help Mrs. Malone with lunch," Mrs. Spencer said as she approached. Jimmy left quickly for the servants' quarters and Mrs. Spencer began to close the double doors to the library. "Oh, forgive me, Mrs. Hamilton. I didn't know anyone was in here. Violet fell asleep in my arms so I laid her in the cradle."

"I am grateful to you, Mrs. Spencer. Um—I have just learned that Jimmy is afraid to come into the library," Mary said.

Mrs. Spencer nodded. "He's been that way since he first came to work here, Madam. I've tried to tell him there is nothing to fear. The boy has a vivid imagination."

"I see," said Mary. "I am going upstairs to check on Clara now. Will you set tea for us in the upstairs sitting room?"

"Miss Clara is already having her tea in the drawing room," explained Mrs. Spencer. As she was speaking, Clara emerged from the drawing room and began walking toward them.

"Mary," Clara said quietly. "Thank you for coming back." Mrs. Spencer took it as her cue to let the ladies speak privately.

"I am sorry I left like that," Mary apologized, finding it difficult to look Clara in the eye. "Please forgive me."

"I'm not sure if you will forgive me, Mary. I was in the drawing room just now taking tea with your moth—" Clara barely stopped herself in time, "—with Mrs. Davenport."

Mary tensed up. "She is here right now?"

"Yes, and I think you should hear her out. You may get some answers that will help you. If you'll excuse me, I have to find some documents in the library to discuss with her."

Mary remembered what William and Abigail said about making amends. She felt her teeth clench at the thought of going into the drawing room just then. "I will see her for a moment, but I can't promise I will stay," Mary said reluctantly. She went to the drawing room and lowered herself onto the chaise lounge, the furthest seat from where Mrs. Davenport sat on the sofa. The ticking of the clock was all that was heard for the minutes that felt like hours.

Finally, Mrs. Davenport broke the silence. "I never meant to hurt him, Mary."

Mary crossed her arms over her chest and spoke in a low voice. "Then what did you suppose would happen when you poisoned his drink?" Mary heard the sofa creak like Mrs. Davenport had turned to face her, but Mary did not want to look at her.

"The doctor told me it was a sedative. I never would have dreamed of harming your father."

"So you put drugs in his drink without his knowledge. How is that any better?" Mary asked bitterly.

"I was trying to help," Mrs. Davenport said firmly. "Believe what you will."

"Clara said I should hear you out," Mary said, stiffening her back. "I am only here as a favor to her."

Mrs. Davenport seemed to be getting agitated. "I would tell you, but you don't seem interested in listening to what really happened anyway."

The clock continued ticking loudly. Mary wondered how much longer Clara would be before she returned with the documents from the library. "I will listen," she said at last.

"Your father was not well in those days. It all began when he received news that greatly troubled him. He wouldn't leave his library, and his attendance at meals became sporadic. He started making rash decisions and I was afraid for the state of his mind and the future of our estate. I begged your father to see the doctor, but he refused. That is why I put the sedative in his drink. I hoped it would help him to calm down and return to his former self."

"What was the news that he received?" Mary questioned.

Mrs. Davenport shrugged. "Heaven only knows—he wouldn't tell me. But he insisted he would change his Will and claim the housekeeper's daughter as his heir! I was only trying to save him from himself, and protect the inheritance of our children."

"And then your plan was to send me to a lunatic

hospital once I inherited the estate. I saw the document that Dr. Jones gave you," said Mary.

"Dr. Jones assured me that you would be treated and released within a week's time. You weren't well, Mary, and in no condition to run the estate."

"What about when I was running the estate after that, and you came to take it all away from me by revealing that I was never my father's child? You led Clara to believe that she could claim the estate for herself—but it was all a deception. You were just lying in wait to take everything for yourself."

Mrs. Davenport shrugged again. "I did those things for you, Mary. I couldn't bear to see the estate run into the ground. I knew I could manage it efficiently and even arrange an advantageous marriage for you. I saw no reason why Clara should have gotten everything while you had nothing. I did my best to protect you from the knowledge that she was your father's daughter. I imagined you would only be hurt if you knew the truth. I even offered a great deal of money to her mother so she could start a new life with Clara somewhere else."

"Yes, I heard all about it. When that didn't work, you tried to convince me that Clara was stealing from me so I would send her away," Mary said in disgust. "You took the jewelry yourself!"

"Oh Mary," she said, waving her hand dismissively. "I only took the necklace and brooch you never cared for in the first place. You'll remember that I was sure to save the gold bracelet from your father. I knew it was your favorite. Don't you see that everything I have done is so that you could live a grand life, free from scandal? You could have been wealthy beyond your imagination right now if you married the man I chose for you. Honestly, Mary, I'm surprised you have not been more grateful since you learned that I took you in. You could have been left to die in the streets like so many unwanted children, yet I gave you the life of a privileged daughter. You never wanted for anything while I ran the house."

"You have an answer for everything, don't you? You treated everyone horribly yet you justify it to yourself a hundred ways. I can't believe you have been corresponding with Clara and I never knew a thing about it."

"She kept it from you to spare your feelings. I'm sure you can understand that, Mary. You've done the same to her…or have you finally decided to tell her that you ran into Joe Blake?"

Mary stood up quickly to close the door of the drawing room and turned back to face Mrs. Davenport. "How could you possibly know that?"

Mrs. Davenport shrugged. "I keep an ear out, Mary. It's how anyone survives in this world anymore. You even walked right past me that day as you left the hotel. You seemed too busy to notice."

A sudden look of realization came over Mary's face. "You are the mystery writer for the gossip column, aren't you! I should have known when those stories began to surface that only you would have such condemning information on the townspeople and be happy to use it against them. I'm surprised you didn't use your column to reveal to the world that Joe was in town and make Clara even more upset!"

"The people in my gossip column had it coming, Mary. You need not feel sorry for them at all. But you should know by now that I would never do a thing to bring public scandal on this house. All I have done is try to save it so that you could have a future. I am not here to hurt you or Clara or anyone. I'm here to help."

"Forgive me if I don't believe you. Your actions have meant nothing but misery for Clara and me!"

"How could you say that, Mary? Ever since you came into my home, I did everything for you to have the best in life. Did you know that I dismissed my own attending maid so that we could afford your debutante ball? Oh I suppose I was harsh on Clara all those years because I worried she would take away what was yours. Can't you see that I have done these things for you?"

Mary put her hands on her hips. "I know the truth about my birth and why you took me. I know you lied about being pregnant so your husband wouldn't divorce you! You probably lied about Richard being his child too, now that I think about it."

"How dare you!" Mrs. Davenport said angrily. "I was never unfaithful to James! You have no idea what really happened in those days. If you did, you would never accuse me like this." She turned to face away from Mary and crossed her arms over her chest. "I hoped you would someday appreciate how much I sacrificed for you after your own parents cast you away. I gave you a chance to live better than you possibly could have on the streets."

Mary felt her jaw clench again. "I wasn't cast aside. I was taken forcefully from parents who loved me! I know who my parents are and I know the truth about everything!"

Mrs. Davenport was skeptical. "What do you mean you were taken forcefully? How do you know who your parents are?"

Mary looked at her to study her face. It seemed clear

that Mrs. Davenport was in the dark about Mary's true mother and father. Mary abruptly rose from her seat and left the drawing room. On her way up the grand staircase to her room, she saw the housekeeper arranging the flowers on the hall table. "Mrs. Spencer, where on earth is Clara?" asked Mary impatiently.

"Miss Clara left the house with Jimmy to visit the neighbor," she answered.

Mary was dumbfounded. "Clara left the house? Oh I just don't believe this!" She went to her room and opened the suitcase in which she packed her jewelry box the night before. She removed a folded paper from a hidden compartment of the jewelry box and sat on her bed to read it. Her head was spinning and she needed a moment to remember what was real.

Dearest Anna,

I pray this letter reaches you one day, when you are the fine lady you always deserved to be. Your father worries that he is to blame for not going for the doctor sooner, but it was never his fault. The doctor will not come for me, for he knows my secret and he wishes for the truth to die with me. When your father was imprisoned, I was poor and starving with no way to care for you. That was when the doctor found me. He said that an important lady would raise you in a grand house and that you would want for nothing. I could not give you up, but the doctor took you from me at my weakest moment and instructed the nurse to leave me to die. The nurse would not obey the doctor, and helped me to find you. I arrived at Davenport House the next day and pleaded with the housekeeper to hire me as a nurse for the newborn baby. Mrs. Price showed pity on me when I convinced her that my own baby had died and that I had milk to nurse another. I was hired that moment, and neither Margaret nor anyone in the house knew that I was your true mother. I have loved to be by your side and watch you grow. I love you and your brother dearly. I know you will take care of him after I am gone because I see how much your heart cares for him, already knowing what your mind does not. Tell your father that I love him and that he has never done a thing wrong. I hid from the doctor for years whenever he was in the house, but one day he saw me. Now he refuses to help when he knows I will die. I know I am sinning by keeping it from John that you were not truly lost. I fear that if he discovers the doctor's crimes, John will kill him and be hanged. I have come to peace with your being raised in Davenport House. I wished sometimes that I could take you away, but you are cared for by a kind man. I could not have given you the life that he will. I hope that my family will forgive me for this truth I have withheld. The nurse who helped me was called Anna. I must call you Mary in the house, but I have named you Anna in my heart. With my last breaths I give all my love to John, and to my children, Anna and Ethan.

Truly,

Your Mother

At the Valentis' farmhouse, Clara arrived with Jimmy and proceeded to introduce him to Phillip. "Jimmy is now working at the house, but I thought you might like some help now that he is through with his morning chores."

Phillip looked at Jimmy, then at Clara. "Thank you for the offer, Clara. I could use the help, but if the boy has been working all morning already, I'm not sure I can accept."

"It's all right, Sir. I like doing the work," Jimmy said happily. He began moving the damaged parts of the wall outside the house as he had observed Phillip doing when they got there.

"He seems a good boy," Phillip remarked to Clara. "I could be done with this kitchen in no time if I had someone hauling out the refuse and building up this chimney."

"Then I am glad I brought him over," Clara replied. "Oh Phillip, I just had to get away from the house. I'm afraid I may have done something terrible, but I don't know for certain!"

Phillip laughed. "How can you not know whether you have done something terrible?"

Clara covered her face with her hands. "I invited Mrs. Davenport to the house…and I left Mary alone with her just now!"

"Oh boy," Phillip said with a cringe. "Why did you invite her in? I remember how much trouble she gave you before."

Clara sighed. "It's a long story, and I really should get back to the house before Mary decides never to speak to me again."

"I hope you come back and tell me the story when you have more time. You have me curious now," Phillip said, beginning to welcome a distraction from his labor.

"Then I will return tomorrow," Clara promised. "Who knows, you may be the only person still willing to speak with me by then!" Phillip chuckled as she left the house. He gratefully accepted Jimmy's help with the repairs for the rest of the day.

Back at Davenport House, Mary returned to the drawing room where Mrs. Davenport was still seated on the sofa. "Mary, I did not think you would come back. I'm beginning to think Clara isn't going to return with the documents she left for. I won't disturb either of you any longer." Mrs. Davenport took her cane and rose from the sofa.

"Wait," Mary said, hardly believing that she had uttered a word that could prolong Mrs. Davenport's visit. "Something has been on my mind that I can't make sense of, but I think you know the answer. Who was I named after?"

Mrs. Davenport seemed surprised by the question. "You weren't named after anyone in the family tree. Your father had decided on your name before we ever expected to have a daughter. I agreed in order to make him happy."

Mary looked at her skeptically, then asked her question. "Then whose grave is that on the estate—the one that is not within our family cemetery?"

Mrs. Davenport appeared to grow sad. "That is a big question…but I will answer if it gives you some solace. She deserved a place in the family cemetery, but it was impossible to do so under the circumstances. She is the daughter that I lost while your father was away. I wasn't lying when I told him I was pregnant. I knew that James would be devastated and never forgive himself if he knew I went into labor as soon as his carriage left the drive. He said the only reason he had not divorced me was because I was having his child. It did not stop him from leaving me out of anger that day.

Dr. Jones was there to help me deliver. But the baby died in my arms just after the birth. I lost my husband and our daughter on the same day. I became desperate to give him a daughter so that it might be as if she had lived. Dr. Jones explained that I could adopt a baby girl and my husband would never know the difference. I agreed because I did not know what else to do. The groundskeeper helped me with the baby's burial and I paid him well to keep her grave hidden and secret. I suppose I must have paid him too well, because not long after, he left for another town to start a life with his newfound wealth.

"I was in utter distress over losing the baby, Mary. I worried that your father would return home and accuse me of lying again if I had no child to show for my pregnancy. Yes, I had him believe you were ours. Dr. Jones arranged it all. Like I say, I was desperate nearly to the point of madness. And in my heart I wished it were true—that my daughter was alive. I hope you never know the pain of the loss of a child."

Mary felt hot tears behind her eyes when she considered how it would have felt to lose Violet. She had the urge to check on her just then. "I am returning upstairs," Mary said quietly. "I'm afraid I don't know when Clara will be back to speak with you."

"There is something else you should hear, Mary. I know you partly blame Dr. Jones for what happened to your father, but you should be aware that he has returned to Yorktown…as the resident doctor of the new hospital."

Mary was aghast. "How can that be? I thought he was sentenced to be hanged!"

"He was pardoned, Mary. During the shortage of doctors and able bodies, many prisoners were pardoned because of the War. This makes me no happier than it makes you. I'm still angry with him for deceiving me about what I put in my husband's drink. I wish I would have known what sort of person he was before it was too late."

"Dr. Jones is a murderer and doesn't deserve to live!" cried Mary. "He killed my mother!"

"What? Mary, how could you think such a thing?"

Mary pulled the letter from her pocket and showed it to her. Mrs. Davenport appeared bewildered at first as if she could not tell what she was reading. Then she sank back down into the sofa with eyes wide with horror. She read the letter twice over. It was one of the rare times in her life that Mrs. Davenport was rendered speechless.

"I was never an unwanted child. I was stolen from my own mother," Mary said in resentment.

Mrs. Davenport gave her back the letter. "I never would have agreed to it if I knew about this, of course. Dr. Jones deceived us all."

"And he deserves to pay for his crimes, " Mary said, her voice shaking with emotion. "Surely you can do something about it, now that you know."

"What can I do?"

"You have the ear of everyone who reads the paper. You could have him run out of town, if you really wanted to help," Mary said.

"I—I don't know, Mary," Mrs. Davenport stammered. "The paper has already warned me about saying too much about the townspeople. If I wrote a piece on Dr. Jones, I could lose the column for good."

Mary returned her hands to her hips, her anger toward Mrs. Davenport boiling fiercely. "You were quick enough to threaten William with being run out of town when it suited you—and William was innocent! You could have destroyed my family! How am I supposed to believe that you really care about any of us?"

Mrs. Davenport was unapologetic. "Oh come now, Mary. Did you forget that we were at War with the Germans? You were putting yourself in danger by being involved with him at such a time. Furthermore, he had no means to provide you with any decent standard of living. I was only trying to protect you, just as I have your whole life! "

Mary turned her back on her and was about to exit the room. Mrs. Davenport continued speaking. "I know you resent me for the choices I've made, but I wish you would see that everything I have done is for your benefit. You may see it as overbearing, but I could not help myself once I learned of your condition. You were so sickly as an infant that the doctors did not expect you to live to your first birthday. I did everything I could to keep you safe and indoors where you could not be injured. Oh I could have strangled your father when he got you that horse to ride…"

"What condition are you talking about?" Mary asked, her back still turned to her.

"I took you to every specialist in Pennsylvania and New York. You would often faint and were terribly slow to heal. The doctors said your blood was weak and that even the most trivial injury could be fatal for you."

Mary thought about the scar from her operation. Tears began to fall down her face. "I hear my baby crying upstairs," she murmured. "I must go to her."

As Mary was leaving the drawing room, Clara was about to walk in with the file of documents. "I'm sorry I took so long to return," she apologized to Mary. "Do you understand now why I asked her to come?"

Mary was drained from the conversation that just took place. She wiped her tired eyes and looked sadly at Clara before walking away. "You might trust her…but I don't and never will. I'm sorry, Clara."

CHAPTER 10

"Mr. Valenti is here to see you, Madam," Mrs. Spencer announced to Clara

"He is?" Clara asked in surprise. "Thank you, Mrs. Spencer. Please tell Phillip that I will meet him in the drawing room in just a few moments." She smoothed her hair and dress while checking her reflection in the vanity mirror. She soon arrived in the drawing room to see Phillip, who wore his suit that day.

"Good morning," she greeted him with a giggle. "I hardly recognized you just now."

Phillip gave a shy smile. "I'm going to Pittsburgh today to retrieve Gabriella and Donnie. I just wanted to thank you for sending Jimmy to help with the repairs. We got the chimney finished and the kitchen is done."

"Oh, I am happy for you," Clara said. "You must be anxious to see the children again."

"I sure have missed them," he said with a chuckle. "I never thought I would say this, but it's been too quiet at the house. It will be good to have them back."

They both stood awkwardly for a moment. Clara cleared her throat. "Um—can I see the new kitchen?"

"Oh—you want to see the kitchen? Yes, of course," he stammered.

They walked over to the farmhouse in silence. Clara smiled when they walked in the door and she saw that everything was in its rightful place with little sign of damage. "You have done well," she said. "Thank you for letting me see your finished work."

"Sure," he said. All went quiet again.

"I suppose I should be going now, so you may get on with your journey," Clara said. She was reluctant to leave but did not have a good reason to stay.

"I hope to hear your story sometime, Clara," he said apologetically. "I'm afraid I have to get going if I'm to make the train in time."

"Yes, of course. I wish you safe travels there and back with the children," Clara turned to exit the front door.

"Wait," Phillip said, doing his best to think fast. "Would you—do you maybe want to come with me? Serena will be happy to see you again—and you can tell me what's been happening in the house on the way over."

"I would love to go!" she answered with joy. "I was hoping for an excuse to get away from the house. Mary hardly said a word to me this morning. Let me just go and tell my housekeeper that I'll be away for the rest of day—we can take my car to Pittsburgh! Would that be all right?"

"Sure beats taking the train," he said with a laugh. "I'll wait at the car for you."

On their way to Pittsburgh, Clara relayed the events of the past week. "I hope I was right to communicate with Mrs. Davenport. I only wish that Mary would understand.

It made me realize just how much I care about the estate. I want to carry on with my father's legacy, and I suppose I feel guilty for ever thinking of leaving it." She looked at Phillip who was listening quietly all the while. "Oh dear, I have just realized that all I have done is talk this whole car ride," she said.

Phillip chuckled. "I don't mind. It's helping to keep my mind off seeing my father again. If I took the train like I planned, I'm sure it would be all I was thinking about."

"But Phillip, you really are lucky that both your parents are still living," Clara remarked. "Mother and I had our differences, but in the end, I realized that none of that really mattered as long as we cared for each other. I never knew who my father was until it was too late. How I wish I had the chance to get to know him."

"You haven't met my father," Phillip grumbled. "There isn't a more stubborn person on earth. I'm astounded that he allowed Serena back into the house in the first place… my mother must have talked him into it somehow."

"Perhaps she did…is your mother very persuasive?"

Phillip chuckled again. "She can be. Clara, I hope you don't mind, but I planned to look at some homes to rent while in Pittsburgh. It shouldn't delay us too long, but I did want to view the places before we picked up the children. Would it be all right with you?"

"Of course," Clara said with a hint of sadness. "I forgot that you were considering moving away."

They drove to a neighborhood that made Clara's skin crawl. Phillip parked in front of the house that had a hand-written sign in the window, ROOM FOR RENT. A fight broke out between several men not far away. Clara could hear glass bottles breaking and voices shouting at each other. Phillip looked at Clara while they were still in the parked car. "What do you think? Should we go inside?"

Clara was unsure how to respond. "Can I be honest? When we first drove onto this street, I had a feeling of dread."

Phillip forced a smile and put the car back into drive. "I had the same feeling. I'm glad you said something."

"Then you are not offended?"

"Not at all, Clara. It's important to me that my children are safe when they go outside or walk to school."

The next house they pulled up to was very close to the train station. The walls of the house rattled each time a train passed. "It's better than the last one," Clara said. "Could you tolerate the noise of the trains every day?"

"Might have to," Phillip said, trying to be realistic. The horn of a train passing by sounded off just then, causing both Clara and Phillip to jump. "Let's keep looking," Phillip said with a sigh.

The third room they looked at was furthest from the school. "This one is not so noisy…and I like how it's not too close to the busy part of town," Phillip remarked.

Clara nodded. "Will it do for your future home?"

Phillip shrugged. "I think so. It's similar to the way we lived before we moved into the farmhouse."

"I see. Out of the others we saw today, I suppose this one would be the least objectionable."

Phillip nodded thoughtfully as he continued to look around the house. "We should get going to pick up the children now. Thank you for looking at the houses with me, Clara. I think it helps to have a woman's input on these things."

"I am glad you suggested that I come with you today. I

can't tell you how lovely it feels to get away from the house for a while."

Phillip left his address with the landlord before he and Clara drove to their final stop: his parents' house on the outskirts of Pittsburgh. Serena ran out to greet them as soon as Phillip parked the car in front. "Clara?" she asked in pleasant surprise. "How wonderful of you to come for a visit. I hope you'll stay for supper."

Phillip gave Serena a look. "We just came to pick up the children and go," he said.

"You know our mother would never allow you to leave without eating first," Serena said with a laugh. "Come, Clara. I want to show you my room here." She linked arms with Clara and led her into the house with Phillip following behind.

Gabriella squealed with excitement when she saw them approach. "Miss Clara! You came to my grandma's house!"

"Hello, dear," Clara said, suddenly blushing from the attention.

Mrs. Valenti was in the kitchen when she heard the commotion. She walked out to see Gabriella hugging Clara around the legs and Phillip standing by awkwardly. "Well? Aren't you going to introduce us?" Mrs. Valenti said to her son.

"Clara, this is my mother. Mother…meet Clara."

"I'm pleased to meet you, Mrs. Valenti," Clara said shyly.

"And I am pleased to meet you too. Come have a seat in the kitchen so I can talk to you while I cook."

"Ma," groaned Phillip. "We have just come to take the children back home. I don't think Clara has time to stay and talk."

Mrs. Valenti looked disappointed. "You won't be staying for supper?"

Clara looked between Phillip and his mother. "Oh, I think I can stay a little while."

Mrs. Valenti perked back up. "Wonderful! Now come with me so I can show you how to get the sauce just right." She disappeared with Clara into the kitchen.

Phillip heard Serena giggling behind him. He spun around. "Do you mind telling me what's so funny?"

"Ma is showing Clara her secret recipe as we speak, and you don't see anything funny about that," Serena answered mischievously. "Our mother already made plans for you two the instant you brought Clara into the house. You should stop our mother before she says anything about more grandchildren at the supper table."

Phillip smacked his forehead with his hand. "I was thinking we could just get the children and leave. I should've known better than to bring Clara with me."

"She must have been terribly bored today. You are not all that exciting of a person for conversation," she said with a laugh.

"Come on, help me, Serena," he muttered. "Can you explain to Ma that Clara is only our neighbor? I don't want Ma getting any ideas."

The voice of Mr. Valenti suddenly boomed into the hallway. "Son? What are you doing standing in the hallway? Come out here where I can look at you."

Phillip gave Serena a pathetic look. "Into the lion's den I go," he said dramatically.

Mr. Valenti watched from the sofa as Phillip entered the sitting room. "I hear that you're an American citizen now. Is that true?"

"It's true," Phillip mumbled. He walked close enough to his father to hold out several coins to him.

"What's this for?" asked Mr. Valenti.

"It's the train fare you sent for me. I didn't use it."

"You can keep it anyway, son. Serena tells me you don't have enough money to keep your own house."

Phillip felt his neck stiffen. "Serena talks too much."

Mr. Valenti shrugged. "She sure cares about you though. She explained to us about how you took her in and supported her after…the unfortunate incident."

"It was you who forced her out and left her penniless in the streets," he said bitterly.

"Your mother tells me it was a mistake, and I suppose I agree with her now," Mr. Valenti said, shaking his head. "Sometimes you think do everything to raise your children right, and then something like this happens. You'll see what I mean when Gabriella is grown."

Phillip was insulted by his father's implication. He crossed his arms stubbornly. "I wouldn't let her out of my sight long enough for her to do anything foolish."

Mr. Valenti held his stomach and laughed heartily. "You can't control every action of a daughter, no matter how much you might wish to."

Phillip did not respond, but turned around to head toward the children's bedrooms.

"Where are you going?" asked his father.

"I'm going to get the children. I don't want to impose on you and Ma any longer."

"Wait just a minute, son." Mr. Valenti rose from the sofa and took an envelope from the fireplace mantle. "Take this with you."

Phillip was baffled by the envelope full of cash. "What is this?" he asked.

"It's to pay the taxes on your house…and a little extra," he answered.

"I can't take this," Phillip said, handing it back. "I never earned it."

Mr. Valenti did not take the envelope from Phillip but instead turned to sit back on the sofa. "You'll take it, all right, because you love your children so much you'll do anything for them…even if it means taking money from the man you hate. Serena has already forgiven me. I hope you will too someday."

Phillip swallowed the lump in his throat. "I'll pay you back," he started to say.

"Son, you went to war and fought to become an American and still took care of your family all the while. I heard you nearly lost a limb, too. You've earned it."

Donnie walked into the sitting room just then. "Papa, are we going home now?"

Phillip turned to pick up Donnie and hold him in his arms. "We are going now. We just have to get your sister."

"Gabriella says she's not coming home with us," Donnie said sadly.

Phillip chuckled. "Why would she say that? Don't worry, I'll go talk to her. Stay here with your grandpa for a minute."

"Come here, Donnie," Mr. Valenti said playfully.

Phillip stuffed the envelope into his suit pocket. Before he left the sitting room, he turned to look his father in the eye. "I don't hate you," he said.

Mr. Valenti nodded. "All right, son."

Phillip nodded back and felt a weight lift from him as

he went down the hallway to find Gabriella. She was crying softly in one of the bedrooms.

"Gabriella, what happened?" Phillip asked. He seated himself next to her on the bed.

"I want to go home with you," she whimpered.

"We will leave just as soon as you cheer up. Why did you tell Donnie you didn't want to come back home with us?"

"I thought you didn't want me to come back."

"Gabriella Maria, you are only being silly. Do you think I would drive all this way to come get you, only to leave you behind?"

"But you were so angry when I burned down the house," she said, wiping tears off her face. "It's why you sent me away."

Phillip felt his heart aching for the little girl. "Is that what you were thinking all this while? You didn't burn down the house. The firebox was closed just as it should have been."

"Then what happened?" she asked with wide eyes.

He looked at the ceiling and groaned. "It was my fault. I should have kept the chimney clean, but I did not. That's what caused the fire."

"You burned down the house?" she asked in disbelief..

"Yes, it was me," he laughed. "And even if you did leave the firebox open, I would still want you to come home with me."

Gabriella threw her arms around him. "I will never make you angry again, Papa."

"We all make mistakes," he said, choking on his words. "But I always want you to come home to me no matter what—understand?"

She nodded solemnly. "I understand, Papa."

Phillip held her hand and led her to the kitchen where he planned to retrieve Clara. He opened the kitchen door just in time to see Clara wearing an apron and stirring a pot with a wooden spoon under Mrs. Valenti's guidance. The savory aroma of Italian sauce made Phillip's knees go weak.

Mrs. Valenti gazed at Clara endearingly. "You have such a lovely complexion, Clara. Your children will be very fair."

"We have to go!" Phillip said so loudly and abruptly that it startled the ladies. He gave his mother a hasty kiss on the cheek. "Thank you for taking the children in this week, Ma. I must get them home now."

Mrs. Valenti looked sadly into his eyes. "But our supper is nearly ready, and I can't have my grandchildren starving all the way to York County."

"No one is starving, Ma," he said, only to be betrayed by a loud growl from his stomach. It took all of his willpower to say no to his mother's cooking, but he would make the sacrifice it if it meant avoiding an awkward supper. Phillip took a deep breath. "I must get Clara back to her house. Sorry, Ma."

Clara removed her apron and hung it on the hook near the table. "Thank you, Mrs. Valenti. I will see if I can make this sauce half as well after I get home."

She followed Phillip into the narrow hallway outside the kitchen. "Phillip," she whispered. "I really don't mind staying a little longer."

He looked at her incredulously. "You don't?"

Clara shook her head. "It's all right, truly. If it's too uncomfortable for you, then we can leave now. I just wanted you to know it's not uncomfortable for me." She stifled a giggle when Phillip's stomach growled loudly again.

"I suppose we can stay—so the children at least get one last good meal," he acquiesced. "Once I'm cooking for them again, there are no guarantees."

"I was hoping you'd be staying, son," his father said from behind him. "Are you going to introduce me to this lovely young lady?"

Phillip sighed. "Clara, this is my father. Father…Clara."

"You must be the Clara I've heard so much about from my Serena," said Mr. Valenti.

Clara laughed nervously. "I'm afraid so, Mr. Valenti. I'm pleased to meet you."

He led her back into the kitchen where the whole family proceeded to seat themselves at the small wooden table. Phillip finished his meal before everyone else. He hoped they could leave before anything embarrassing could be said, but it was evident that he was the only one in a hurry to go. The whole family seemed to be enjoying Clara's company, and she theirs. After supper, the family went outside to say goodbye to Phillip, Clara, and the children.

Mrs. Valenti took her son aside. "I have something for you to give Clara," she said discreetly. She handed him a gold ring from her apron pocket.

Phillip looked around quickly to make sure no one had heard or seen. "Ma, it's not like that," he insisted. "Didn't Serena explain to you that Clara is only our neighbor?"

"Serena never said any such thing," his mother said, looking confused. Phillip glared at Serena, who responded with a smirk. "Why would you bring your neighbor here to meet the family if it wasn't more than that?"

"It—it's a long story," he stammered.

"Ever since Serena arrived, she told us such

wonderful things about this Clara. Why don't you take her for a wife already?"

"She doesn't even think about me like that," he replied.

"Of course she does," his mother said with confidence. "My son is strong and handsome and a hero of this fine country."

Phillip thought hard about what he could say to dissuade his mother from pursuing the subject. Finally he knew the answer. "Clara is not Catholic."

Mrs. Valenti went speechless for a moment. "I see. She might convert, you know."

"Ma, I'm sorry it wasn't what you thought with Clara and me, but we really have to leave now."

"Very well," Mrs. Valenti said sorrowfully. "Give your mother a kiss first." He gave her a peck on the cheek while she hugged him tightly.

"Goodbye, Ma."

The car ride back to Pittsburgh was quiet. Clara glanced into the backseat at Gabriella and Donnie. "The children are asleep," she told Phillip quietly.

"It's been a long day," he sighed. "I'm really sorry for keeping you out so long."

"It was a lovely dinner. It was very kind of Serena to tell your parents such nice things about me."

"It was well-deserved, I'm sure," Phillip said. "Uh—Clara—my parents seemed to have made up their minds that you and I had an understanding—and that I was bringing you home to meet them. I'm sorry if anything they said to you was improper."

"You really must stop apologizing, Phillip," she responded. "It was the most fun I've had in a long time. Honestly."

They sat in silence for the rest of the drive home. When they arrived at the farmhouse, Clara helped put the children to bed.

Gabriella looked at her father sleepily. "The city was so noisy, Papa. I am glad we are home now so we can sleep all night."

"But the city is not so bad, is it?" he asked her. "Wouldn't you like to try living there sometime?"

Gabriella shook her head. "There was nowhere for me and Donnie to play except in the house. I missed our property…and having Miss Clara for a neighbor."

"Me too," said Donnie.

"Now that you are home in your own bed, it is time for sleep," said Phillip. "Goodnight."

"Goodnight, Papa," they replied.

On the short drive over to Davenport House, Clara spoke to Phillip. "The next time you visit your family in Pittsburgh and want some company, I hope you'll ask me."

"Sure I will," replied Phillip. "I suppose it wasn't so bad after all. You know, that wasn't the first time we drove to Pittsburgh together. Do you remember?"

Clara thought back. "I can't remember. Why did we go?"

"You had an address you wanted me to take you to. It wasn't far from my parents' house where we just visited. I remember it well because you seemed anxious on that trip, especially after you spoke to the man at the door." Phillip could feel himself turning red, but he finished his story anyway. "You held onto me all the way back to the car. I felt so angry at whoever had made you that upset, but it wasn't my place to speak up about it. I wished I could have done something to help."

"I remember now," she said quietly. "It was an address where Lawrence was having his mail sent. I was such a fool to trust him."

Phillip parked the car in its rightful place in front of the house. Clara seemed distraught when he opened her door and walked her to the front steps. "I'm sorry, Clara. Maybe I shouldn't have mentioned that day."

"Oh—no—I'm not upset about that," Clara stuttered, her voice catching in her throat. "I've just noticed that Mary's car is gone. She would not still be out this late unless she decided to stay with William at the clinic. What if she cannot forgive me?"

"I'm sorry, Clara. If you need someone to talk to, you know I'll be just next door."

"Thank you," she whispered. "Goodnight, Phillip."

"Goodnight," he answered. He watched her walk through the entrance of the imposing house, then he walked back to his home. He was relieved to finally remove his suit jacket and begin to relax for the day. He hung his jacket over the bureau and reached into the pocket for the envelope that his father had given him. As he was counting the money, a shiny metal object between the bills caught his eye. He carefully took it out and looked at it in the candlelight. It was his mother's ring.

In the city of Yorktown, Mary was parking her car in front of the new hospital. Her heart felt like it might beat out of her chest, but she was determined to go inside. She climbed out of her car in the dark and approached the entrance of the hospital. Her stomach turned when she saw Dr. Jones through the clear windows. He was sitting behind a desk and looking over ledgers. Mary knocked on the glass door. Dr. Jones looked up from the ledgers and went to open the door for her.

"Mary," he said in bewilderment, yet smiling with his teeth. "Or I suppose I should address you as 'Mrs. Hamilton' now. Things have certainly changed in the last five years, haven't they? You must be here to check out the competition." He laughed nervously.

Mary pushed past him into the hospital, feeling her heart pounding loudly in her ears. "No Dr. Jones, I have not come here to check out the competition. I have come for a different reason entirely."

Chapter 11

The next morning at Davenport House, Clara dined at the breakfast table alone. She wondered if it was the life she should be getting used to—a life without Mary in the house. She was glad to hear footsteps approaching the dining room. "William!" she said in surprise. "It's been ages since you had breakfast with us. You must have arrived late last night."

William looked tired as though it had been awhile since he last slept. "No, I just arrived. Have you seen Mary this morning? I thought she would be in here having breakfast."

"Usually she is, but I haven't seen her. I thought she was with you."

"No, she wasn't with me," William said. "I'll go upstairs to see her. I have some news."

"Good morning," Mary said cheerfully as she entered the dining room. "William, hello." She stood on her tiptoes and put her arms around his neck. "I've missed you."

"I've missed you too," he said, holding her close. "Something happened in town. It's rather morbid, but it could mean change for us."

Mary went to the buffet and piled her plate high with breakfast foods. "What happened in town?" she asked as she sat down to eat.

"Perhaps I should have waited until you had already eaten to tell you the news," William said quietly.

"You can tell me now," she said. "Forgive me, William. I am starved."

William sighed heavily. "I didn't know how to tell you this, but Dr. Jones, your family doctor from before, came back into town some days ago."

Mary groaned. "Don't worry, William. I was already made aware. Is that all the news you have?"

"No, there is more," he said. "This morning, Dr. Jones was found dead in the new hospital."

Mary shrugged as she focused on her plate. "Pity it didn't happen sooner."

"Mary!" gasped Clara. "It's a sin to speak ill of the dead."

Mary ignored her comment. "Surely the board of directors will want you to work for them now, William. They'll need a new doctor."

William was taken aback by her flippancy. "I imagine the board will be asking me to fill in shortly. I thought you would want to know."

"I'm sure you will get the position, William. You deserve it more than anyone," Mary said between mouthfuls of food.

William served a plate for himself but did not sit at the table. "I can't stay long. I'm going upstairs to see our daughter."

After William left the room, Clara watched Mary as she finished her large plate. Mary looked up at her. "Why are you looking at me like that?" she asked.

"You seem different today. Are you feeling all right?"

Mary smiled. "I am feeling very well, thank you."

Clara managed a smile. "That's good to hear, Mary. I'm at least grateful that you are still speaking to me…after I invited your mother here to talk."

"I can't say I'm happy about it, Clara. I'm worried that she has come to take advantage of you at a vulnerable time, and that you are too good-natured to see it."

Clara looked at her plate and said, "In her letter, she apologized for how she treated me and Mother in the past. I nearly fainted when I read it. I could not believe she said it. Did you ever know her to truly apologize—to anyone—for anything?"

Mary thought about it. "I don't think she has. At least not to me." She rose from her seat and walked around the table to kiss Clara on the cheek. "I just want you to be all right, Clara. I do love you like a sister, you know."

Clara felt her heart jump at Mary's words. "Thank you. I can't tell you how much I needed to hear that today."

In the city of Yorktown, a detective called Giovanni visited William at the clinic. "Dr. Hamilton," he began. "You have probably heard the news about Dr. Jones."

"I have," William answered solemnly.

"A police investigation of the death is underway and we hoped that you would perform the autopsy."

"Of course. I am at your service," William said. He followed Giovanni to the new hospital and met the police chief at the scene.

"Good afternoon, Dr. Hamilton," Chief Reynolds greeted him. "I'm sorry to call you over on such dreary business. We are sure there are signs of struggle, but we want your input on what could have been used as the murder weapon."

"Murder?" William asked. "Do you have a suspect?"

"We haven't gotten quite that far in the investigation. I'm afraid we'll have our work cut out for us once we do. Apparently, the doctor had a good many enemies," answered the chief.

"I see," said William. After performing his examination of the body, he returned to the chief, who stood with Giovanni at the desk by the hospital entrance.

"Well Doctor, what do you think?" the chief asked.

"I've written my findings here," William said, handing him a paper. "Skull fracture, blunt force trauma to the head."

The chief skimmed over the paper. "Thank you. We don't have much to go on at this point, but it's certain the death is suspicious. We think it may have been one of his own patients."

William raised his eyebrows. "That's—terrifying," he said. "Why do you suspect a patient?"

Giovanni held out a book to show him. "Here is the patient sign-in register. The page from yesterday has been torn out of the register and is nowhere to be found. The only other thing out of place is this piece of lady's jewelry. It could have been left by anyone really, but since the hospital just opened days ago, it should not be too hard to locate the owner."

William immediately recognized the gold bracelet on the desk as being identical to one that Mary had. "I should be getting back to the clinic now, if you are finished with my services," he said.

"That should be all, Dr. Hamilton," answered Giovanni. "Thank you for your help."

Back at Davenport House, Mary had just laid Violet down to sleep and was heading downstairs to the library. She saw Jimmy washing the marble floors at the bottom of the staircase.

" 'Afternoon, Mrs. Hamilton," he said with a smile.

"Good afternoon, dear," she replied. Jimmy's cheerfulness was often contagious and Mary found herself smiling when he was near. "How are you enjoying your work here, Jimmy?"

"I like it, Ma'am. This is the grandest house I've ever been in. It's an honor to keep it clean and sparkly."

"And you are doing a lovely job," Mary told him. "I'm going into the library now and I wondered if you might like to have a look inside. You'll need to go into the library to clean eventually. The bookshelves get very dusty, you see. I am in there nearly every day and I promise it's nothing to be afraid of."

Jimmy shrugged with reluctance. "If you insist, Mrs. Hamilton. I will go into the library with you."

She led him through the double doors and watched him gaze in awe at the rows of books. "Well Jimmy, what do you think?"

"It's a lot bigger than I thought it would be," he said, then pointed to a bookcase. "Is that the one with the secret door behind it?"

Mary giggled. "Not that one. I will show it to you. Did Mrs. Spencer tell you about the corridor?"

"No Ma'am. When I mentioned it to Mrs. Spencer, she didn't know what I was talking about. She thought I was making it up."

"Oh," Mary said, furrowing her brow. "Then how did you know about it?" She reached into the bookcase and pulled the metal latch, causing the bookcase to swing away from the wall.

"My grandmother told me about it," Jimmy said. "Can I see the inside?"

"Of course," Mary said slowly. "I will show you where it comes out on the other end. I used to love to play in here when I was about your age." As they walked through the corridor, Mary wondered how Jimmy's grandmother would have known about it. After they made it through the other side, Mary asked him, "How do you suppose your grandmother knew about the passageway?"

"My grandmother knows everything about this house, Ma'am. She used to live here," answered Jimmy.

Mary looked at him curiously. "What is your grandmother's name?"

Jimmy squinted his eyes as if trying to remember. "I don't know her name, Ma'am. I just call her 'Grandmother'."

"Of course," said Mary. They returned to the bottom of the staircase where Jimmy resumed his scrubbing of the floors. Mary was about to go upstairs, but she couldn't stop thinking about the things the servant boy had told her. She turned again to Jimmy, who was humming contentedly as he dried the floor with a linen. "Jimmy, what is your surname?"

He stood up from the floor and wiped his hands on the sides of his pants. "My surname is Davenport, Ma'am. Same as Miss Clara's."

Mary was nearly speechless as she wondered how it could be possible. "Who are your parents?" she questioned.

Jimmy hung his head. "Grandmother said that my

father fought in the War, but he didn't come back. Mother died after getting real sick. So my grandmother took care of me…but then she got real sick too."

"I am sorry about your parents," Mary said compassionately, but she was no less bewildered by his responses. "I'm proud of you for going into the library with me today."

"Thank you for showing me the secret passageway, Ma'am. I suppose that library isn't so bad after all."

Mary went up the stairs and passed Mrs. Spencer in the hallway. "Mrs. Spencer," she began. "I just showed Jimmy around the library."

"Oh, I'm glad you managed to persuade him. He had so many stories about the library, but he was still too scared to step inside."

"Where did you find Jimmy when you hired him?" Mary questioned.

Mrs. Spencer smiled to remember it. "He was hired at Miss Clara's request."

"Clara requested that you hire Jimmy—specifically?"

"Yes, Madam," she answered. "She is taking tea in the upstairs sitting room just now. Would you like to join her?"

"Yes, Mrs. Spencer. I will join Clara in just a moment." Mary went to her bedroom where the family Bible still lay on her nightstand. She looked through the register of relatives' names several times in an attempt to discover if Jimmy could be right about being a Davenport. She could not find answers in all her searching. She tucked the family Bible under her arm and went into the sitting room where Clara sat in front of the fireplace. Clara appeared to be deep in thought.

"Good afternoon, Mary," she said quietly.

"Good afternoon," Mary replied. She sat on the

settee next to Clara. "I just had the strangest conversation with Jimmy."

Clara smiled endearingly. "He is a darling, isn't he?"

"Yes certainly," Mary said quickly. "But do you know who he is?"

"Of course I know who he is," Clara answered. "I thought you did too."

"I have no idea," Mary said. "Jimmy claims to be a Davenport and he seems to know things about this house—well that no one else could know. I just don't see how it's possible."

"Jimmy is Richard's son…which also makes him my nephew," Clara replied.

Mary was stunned. "How did you find out about him?"

"It's what I've been trying to tell you, Mary. Your mother explained everything in her letter to me. I thought she must have told you when she was here the other day."

"She never said a thing about Jimmy," Mary said, her mind still racing to process the revelation.

"I will get the letter from my room. It's time you read it for yourself so you understand why I am doing what I am." Clara returned shortly with several folded papers. Mary took them from her and began to read.

Clara,

You must be surprised to hear from me at a time like this, but the real estate office is under instruction to notify me if Davenport House goes to sale. I have just learned of your intentions to sell but I must urge you not to sell the house or any part of the estate. Our country is heading into terrible times such as it has never seen before. Your estate will sustain you during these hard times, but only if you take measures to expand now and keep it profitable. The riots on Wall Street are just the beginning of widespread financial hardship. You might think that things seem bad now in town with the unemployment line, but they will only get worse in the coming years.

You likely question my motives for cautioning you in this matter. The truth is that I need something from you. It involves my grandson, your own nephew, whom you have never heard of. I saw to it that no one knew of Richard's son born out of wedlock. The boy's mother passed on from influenza and I have been raising him on my own ever since. I cannot care for him in my current circumstances as I have recently moved into a hotel room in the Yorktown Inn. Jimmy is all I have left of my family. I must leave him in capable hands and that is why I am writing you today. I will give you plans for development that will make the estate flourish. I only ask that my grandson be cared for in your house. He already knows the meaning of hard work. I would not object to you taking him on as a servant while you decide what role he is to have in the house, but I think you will understand the importance of family the instant you meet Jimmy. Provide a home for my grandson and I will advise you on how to make your holdings last a lifetime.

I was very sorry to hear about your mother's passing.

Mrs. Price was as much a part of the house as any of the family. I regret my actions toward the both of you and I hope you will accept my apology and condolences.

Regards,

Margaret Davenport

Mary shook her head in disbelief. "This is shocking," she said quietly. "If she is good at anything, it is keeping secrets."

"The letter came to me when I was very low. I was devastated after Joe abandoned me. I did not feel that I had any purpose to live for. But when I learned about Jimmy, I thought I could have purpose again. My mother and father are gone, leaving me with no family to speak of. At least, that is what I thought. The reason I hired Jimmy as a servant was so he could experience the other side of what it's like to live in the house. I don't want him to take anything for granted once I decide to move him upstairs."

Mary was skeptical. "But what if this is just another way that she is trying to gain control of the estate? Jimmy might not even be who she says he is."

"Mary," Clara said gently, laying her hand on Mary's. "I believe he is. Look into his eyes and tell me if you don't see my father in them."

"I suppose I didn't notice," Mary said. "I'm not sure what to think about any of this."

"It's all right. Do you remember the day you met Mrs. Davenport outside the house?"

Mary groaned under her breath. "How could I forget."

"She was coming to tell me that Joe's estate went up for sale. She urged me to do whatever I could to buy it and expand the estate to its original size of a thousand acres."

"And…did you?" asked Mary.

Clara nodded proudly. "It wasn't easy, but Mrs. Davenport helped me with it all. I don't believe she wants the house for herself any longer, Mary. I think she is only concerned that Jimmy is taken care of."

Mary was still skeptical, but held her peace. Clara sighed loudly just then. "Oh, I am so glad you know everything now," she said. "I don't wish for there to be any secrets between us. I'm sorry I was not forthright about it from the start. I was so worried you wouldn't understand."

Mary felt the same pang of guilt that she spent each day pushing to the back of her thoughts. She finally spoke up before she lost the courage to tell her. "Clara, there is a secret I've kept from you as well. I'm worried that if I tell you now that I knew all along, you might banish me forever."

Clara laughed. "Oh Mary, don't be ridiculous. You will always have a home here. But what is this secret? You have me in suspense."

Mary took a deep breath. "I know why Joe left."

Clara's face fell. "You needn't waste your time, Mary. I already know why he left," she whispered.

"You do?"

Clara nodded sadly. "He often spoke of wanting a big family. I told him I would likely never have any children and it was too much a disappointment for him to go through with it. I suppose all this grief could have been avoided if I had just told him sooner."

Mary shook her head dismissively. "Clara—I saw Joe.

He was in Yorktown last week. And that's not the reason he gave me."

Clara's mouth dropped open. "Joe came back to town?"

"Yes," Mary answered gently. "I'm sorry I never told you before, but I was afraid it would hurt you too much to know the truth. Several years ago, Joe knew a young woman…and they had a child."

The color drained from Clara's face until she was white as a sheet. "I can't believe this! He never told me any such thing!"

"Apparently, Joe never knew about the child until recently when he went to see the woman in Harrisburg. He married her within the week."

Clara put her hand over her heart. "I never thought he could be married. I suppose I figured he would not come back to me, but for him to be married so soon…and with no explanation to me! Oh Mary, what a great mistake I nearly made in marrying him! Thank goodness he left when he did. The devastation of me being betrayed after the wedding would be more than I could bear."

"I am terribly sorry about all this, Clara. You deserve so much better."

Clara laid back against the settee. "But Mary, is there anyone in the world would want to be with a woman who has been engaged and married as much as I have? I would die of embarrassment just to explain it all to a man."

"All I know is that you deserve better," said Mary. "Heaven help the man would betray you after this."

Later that night, William pulled into the front drive at Davenport House. He was tired after the long day but determined not to spend another consecutive night away from his wife and daughter. Sam met him outside where the cars were parked in a row. " 'Evening, Dr. Hamilton," Sam told him. "I haven't seen you here for awhile. I've been cleaning the cars real good and I can get yours done in the morning, if you'd like."

"I would appreciate that, Sam," William answered sleepily.

"I found something in Mrs. Hamilton's car that I thought might be yours," Sam continued. "It looks important like that doctor stuff you keep in your car sometimes." Sam reached into his pocket and handed William a sheet of paper.

William looked over it with his tired eyes that suddenly grew wide. He felt his heart drop into his stomach when he realized the significance of what he held in his hand: a page torn from the register of the Yorktown hospital. He looked in horror at the final name handwritten on the register:

Mary Hamilton of Davenport House, "After Hours" Visit

Chapter 12

Phillip Valenti and his children gathered near the garden to collect the few crops that had surfaced that year. Gabriella frowned at the meager harvest. "We could eat all that in one day," she said.

"We likely could, but we'll try to make it last just a little longer than a day," her father answered.

"Miss Clara is coming for a visit," Donnie announced, looking in the distance.

"She is?" Phillip looked up from the garden. Clara was approaching with two baskets full of vegetables.

"Hello," she said to the children. "Do you suppose you could use any of this? We don't have any more room in our cellar."

"We can use them!" Gabriella said joyfully. "Our garden died this year."

Phillip coughed awkwardly. "Well, it didn't do as well as we'd hoped," he said. "Children, what do you say to Miss Clara?"

"Thank you," the children said in unison. Phillip and

Clara watched as they made their way to the house with the heavy baskets.

After the children had gone inside, Clara looked at Phillip. "I wanted to tell you that Mary came back. She did not leave me as I feared. In fact, we seem to be on very good terms now."

"I'm glad to hear it," Phillip said.

"There is something else," she began shyly. "You were right—what you said about Joe. I learned that he has a child with a woman from his past. They are married now."

Phillip shook his head. "And he couldn't be bothered to tell you about this before?"

"He never mentioned it. In fact it was just yesterday that I found out through Mary what truly happened."

"Will you be all right?"

Clara shrugged. "I'm sure I will be. I used to believe that the only way for me to be respected in this world was to be married. But the last weeks have shown me that I can have purpose without it. Your sister wrote me a lovely letter about the difference I made for her before she left for Pittsburgh. Now with Jimmy at the house, I feel more purpose than ever to continue with my father's estate. I don't require a husband to do so. And come November, I will be voting in my very first election," she said, beaming with pride. "Can you believe it?"

Phillip chuckled. "After all the work you put in with the suffrage movement, I can believe it."

Clara saw the children leave the house to play in the backyard. She felt herself becoming sad to watch them. "Do you think you'll hear back from the landlord about the house for rent?"

Phillip seemed confused. "What? Oh, that. If I do hear back from him, I'll have to decline."

"Did you find something better?" she asked.

Philip smiled sheepishly. "I suppose I found a way to stay here at the farmhouse."

"Oh, that's excellent news! How did you manage it?"

"It involved swallowing my pride a little," he said with a laugh. "But I would do it again if it meant giving the children the best I can. When you and I were looking at those houses around Pittsburgh, I suppose I was reminded of the reasons I wanted to live in the country in the first place. I decided I'm going to find a way to make it work for as long as I can right here."

"I am very glad you will be staying. I was going to miss you terribly. After everything that has happened at the house these last years, you've been here for us, the most perfect neighbor we could ask for." Clara suddenly felt embarrassed. "Well, I suppose I should leave you to your harvest."

"Wait," Phillip said, looking up into her eyes. "Thank you for the vegetables, Clara. You have truly been the kindest neighbor we could hope for. The children adore you, you know."

Clara blushed. "You're welcome. Good day, Phillip."

Back at Davenport House, Mary was laying Violet down to sleep in the wooden cradle. She saw William enter the dark room, but could not see his distressed expression.

"Mary, I need to speak with you," he said.

"We'll need to leave the room," whispered Mary. "I just got her to sleep." She went to the hallway with William and looked at him expectantly. "What is it?"

William looked in both directions around them. "I don't want to talk out here in the hallway."

"Oh dear, is it serious? We can go into the sitting room. There is no one there just now." William followed her to the sitting room and closed the double doors while Mary seated herself on the settee. "Is this about the new hospital?" she asked.

"Y—yes—" he stammered. "How did you know?"

"I hoped you had heard back from the directors about a position there."

"No, I haven't heard from them. Mary, have you actually gone inside the hospital?"

"Me?" she laughed. "I have no reason to go in there… especially since I learned about that awful Dr. Jones working there."

"So you've never gone to see Dr. Jones since he got back to town?" William questioned.

Mary was bewildered. "Gone to see him? Of course not! William, I hate that man more than anything in the world. You remember he killed my mother, don't you? Why would you ask such a question?"

William felt nauseated when he replied. "The detective asked me to do the autopsy on Dr. Jones. They think it was a murder."

"More than likely," Mary remarked. "But I hope you don't expect me to feel sorry for him."

"I don't expect you to Mary—it's just that I had to hear from your own lips that you were never there. The police found a gold bracelet that looks just like yours. They might use it for evidence."

"My bracelet from Father is one of my most prized possessions. I would never leave it lying around anywhere. It's safe in my jewelry box at the moment," she assured him.

William breathed a sigh of relief and pushed the feelings

of doubt to the back of his mind. "I'm sorry, Mary. I got so worried and didn't know what to think."

"It must have been distressing to have to do the autopsy," Mary said compassionately. She stood up and hugged him. "I promise I've never stepped foot into that hospital."

"All right," he said. "I'm going to get changed and head back to town now."

"Have a good day, William," she said, stifling a yawn. "I am going downstairs to the library."

William watched her leave the sitting room and head down the grand staircase. William returned to their shared bedroom where Violet was sleeping soundly. He changed his clothes as quietly as he could so he did not wake her up. On his way out the door, he noticed Mary's jewelry box on her vanity table. He held his breath as he opened the box to look inside. He searched through every piece, but the gold bracelet was not there.

In the city of Yorktown, William sat at his desk in the clinic and made a call to the manor house in Philadelphia. "Hello?" answered Abigail.

"Abigail, it's me, William."

"Hello, William. How are you?"

"I'm having difficulty with something and I'm hoping you can help," he said. "Mary has not been herself lately. I don't understand what's happening with her, but I wondered if she might have told you anything. I don't mean to pry—I'm just desperate for answers."

"Oh dear," Abigail said. "Poor Mary has been in distress since she saw her mother again, and she phoned me this morning to say that she is kept awake by nightmares."

"Nightmares? She never mentioned it," William said. "Did she say what about?"

"She only told me she is afraid to return to sleep after having them. Perhaps I left her too soon. But surely you've found a nanny by now."

"No, we are not going to have a nanny," William replied.

"What do you mean? Didn't Mary advertise for help with the baby?"

"She was going to, but I told Mary that she should get accustomed to life without servants. She doesn't believe she can do it on her own, but I think she'll find out she is capable soon enough."

"William, how could you!" scolded Abigail. "Mary is in no condition to be doing everything herself! She should be resting so she can heal."

William was puzzled. "Heal from what? Did something happen?"

Abigail hesitated on the other end. "Mary promised that she would tell you, but from this conversation, I'm afraid she has not. Mary is still in tremendous pain from the birth. She has not healed as she should have. I thought you must have known by now. You'll need to examine her yourself and see what can be done for her. I would have stayed longer to help Mary, but I had to come home."

William leaned his forehead against his arm on the desk. "I had no idea of any of this," he said sorrowfully. "I feel ashamed, Abigail. I have neglected Mary without realizing it and now she doesn't think she can be honest with me."

"Then I hope you find the time to really talk to each other. Do you think I should return to her? I assumed she had someone to help with the baby all this while."

"Yes Abigail, please come. I don't know what's happening with Mary, but there is more that she is not telling me. I'm just afraid to find out what it is."

Chapter 13

"Thank you for your offer, Sir," William said to the director of the hospital. "I'll need to speak with my wife about it first."

The director chuckled knowingly. "Of course you will. Let me know just as soon as you've made your decision, Dr. Hamilton."

"I will, Sir," William replied, shaking the man's hand. He left the hospital and saw Clara's car parked nearby with Sam in the driver's seat. William went to speak with him. "Good morning, Sam. How is everything at the house?"

"It's all right, Dr. Hamilton. Miss Clara seems to be much more herself now," he answered with a smile. "She's out shopping for hats."

"That's good to hear—but I have a favor to ask of you," began William. "Well, it's more a favor to ask of your wife. I hoped you could relay the request to her as soon as you get back to the estate."

"Sure, I'll ask her," replied Sam.

"I understand that Fiona gave up her position at the grand house due to her condition," William said.

"That's right. Keeping up the whole mansion was getting to be too much for her, so now she's staying home while we wait for the baby."

"Of course. I just wonder if she might be able to help Mary with Violet for a few weeks. I'm afraid I can't pay much in cash, but perhaps we can make it up in trade. You can have this or get a good price for it at a second-hand shop. It's Swiss made." William removed his watch.

"I can't take your watch, Dr. Hamilton," Sam told him. "I think if I talk to Fiona, she'd be happy to help your wife for free."

"Are you sure you can do without payment?" asked William, still holding his watch out for Sam.

"Fiona plans to ask Mrs. Hamilton to be her midwife anyway, so I'm sure things will even out in the end."

William sighed humbly. "Thank you, Sam. I am grateful to the both of you."

Later that morning at Davenport House, Clara and Mary were having tea in the upstairs sitting room. "Abigail telephoned this morning," Clara said. "She is coming for another visit."

"How wonderful," responded Mary. "So much has happened since she was here last."

"Morning paper for you, Madam," Mrs. Spencer said, handing Clara the newspaper.

"Thank you, Mrs. Spencer." Clara's eyes went directly to the gossip column. She raised her eyebrows and read with interest.

"What is it?" asked Mary.

"I'm not sure if you want to hear this," she answered slowly. "It's about Dr. Jones."

Mary shuddered. "You just reminded me of the terrible

dream I had last night. You're right, Clara. I don't want to hear any news about him. I have to tend to Violet anyway." She rose from her seat and left the sitting room.

Mary was about to return to her room, but Mrs. Spencer approached her first. "Fiona is here to see you, Mrs. Hamilton."

Mary became concerned. "I hope all is well with the baby."

"She said she is here to help with Violet, Madam."

"She is?" Mary asked in surprise. Mrs. Spencer led her to the parlor where Fiona waited patiently.

"Hello, Miss Mary," Fiona said cheerfully. "Dr. Hamilton sent me to help with the baby. I can arrive every day about this time after breakfast, if it's all right with you."

"Of course it would be all right!" said Mary in delight. "I'm surprised it was William who sent you, but I'm pleased nonetheless. Violet is upstairs in my room just now. She is certainly about to wake up soon."

Fiona smiled sweetly. "I will go attend to her, Miss Mary. You look like you could use some rest."

After Fiona went upstairs, Mary enjoyed a leisurely walk to the stable to see her horse Dolly. "How are you, old friend?" she whispered, running her hand down Dolly's nose. "I wish I could take you for a ride today. It would be just the thing to clear my head."

"Mary?" William's voice called from behind her.

Mary smiled and went to hug him. "Thank you for sending Fiona. It means the world to me."

"Of course," he said, kissing her hair. "I'm sorry I was not more understanding about you needing help."

"How did you manage to come home at this time of day?" asked Mary.

William took a deep breath. "There are things we need to discuss that can't wait any longer."

She sat down with him on a bale of hay in the stable. "I'm listening."

"The board of directors offered me the position at the hospital. It would mean a regular salary but I'll be required to work late often."

Mary shrugged. "I guess we are already used to that. Violet and I will come visit you in town as much as we can."

"But Mary, I fear we are strangers already. I've neglected you and our baby, and I'm very sorry for it."

"You needn't be sorry. I understand."

William swallowed painfully. "You can tell me anything. No matter how bad it is. I just want you to be honest with me."

She looked at him curiously. "How have I not been honest with you?"

"About the new hospital. I know you went there."

Mary stood up from the haystack. "William, I already swore to you that I never stepped foot inside that hospital. Why don't you believe me?"

William clutched his stomach in agony. "The police showed me the patient register at the hospital. The last page was torn from it and missing." William pulled the paper from his pocket and held it out to her. "So tell me what I should think about this."

Mary skimmed the page and sucked her breath in sharply when she read her name. "I don't know why my name is on here or who could have written it. Is that why you took the page from the register? Because you thought I was somehow involved and you were trying to protect me?"

William looked at her in disbelief. "I didn't take the page, Mary. Sam found it—in your car."

"My car?" Mary sat back down on the hay. "This is terrible."

William's voice cracked emotionally. "I just need you to tell me the truth! If you went to the hospital that night, just tell me. I can't tell you how badly I want to throw this paper into the fire and forget that I ever saw it!"

"But I am telling the truth!" she insisted. "William, someone must be trying to implicate me! After our conversation yesterday, I went to my jewelry box for my gold bracelet to wear, and it was gone!"

"You think someone wrote your name on this paper, put it in your car, and stole your bracelet?"

"It has to be," cried Mary. "There is no other possible explanation!"

"Who could have access to the house to do such a thing?" William questioned. He was desperate to believe that Mary had been framed.

A sudden look of realization crossed Mary's face. "It was her! It was Mrs. Davenport! She was in our house! Oh, I just knew we couldn't trust her!"

"That woman is even more despicable than I imagined if she could put her daughter in a situation like this," William said bitterly. "I think we should explain to the police right away. Then I can take the job at the hospital with a clear conscience. Clara can attest that you were at the house with her all night, can't she?"

Mary thought back and frowned. "That was the day Clara went to Pittsburgh. I did not see her until the next morning."

"Then the servants can confirm that you were here at the house," William said.

Mary furrowed her brow. "I—I don't know. It's the strangest thing, but now I can't remember anything about that day…only that Clara left for Pittsburgh. I must have been here. Oh William, I've been such a wreck lately. I can hardly think straight anymore!"

William looked at her with guilt. "I spoke to Abigail on the telephone. She said you are still in pain from the birth. Is that true?"

Mary looked away from him and nodded. "I never wanted you to feel bad about it or think you did something wrong during the operation. But I've learned something about myself…something that Mrs. Davenport said when she was here. She explained that I was a weak child and that I was slow to heal from injuries. She said it was a condition that she took me to specialist doctors for. It's why I faint sometimes. And it's why the incision from the birth never healed over."

"It can't be possible, Mary," William said. "That was months and months ago. It has to be an infection. Let me look."

Mary shook her head. "It's bad, William. I don't want you to see what I look like."

"You should be healed by now. It's scaring me that you're saying you haven't."

Mary closed her eyes and leaned back against the hay stack while William lifted her dress to view the scar. He exhaled deeply in distress and gingerly put her dress back down. "Why didn't you tell me?" he said with his head in his hands. "I would have done anything to make sure you were able to rest." He lifted her up from the haystack and carried her away from the stable.

"What are you doing?" asked Mary, suddenly feeling embarrassed. "I can walk back to the house."

William continued to carry her to the house and up the front steps. "I'm going to close down the clinic. I'll take time off before I accept the new position—while we figure out how to help you with your condition. I have a doctor friend in Philadelphia who knows about this sort of thing."

Mary did not want to argue. She felt great relief in knowing that she could rest in bed without having to feel guilty. William carried her to their bedroom and laid her on the bed. He then lay down beside her. "How painful is it, Mary?" he asked. "I'm going to get you medicine to lessen your symptoms, but I don't want to give too much or too little."

"Does it have to be with a needle?" Mary asked squeamishly. "I'm terrified of needles."

"No, it does not need to be an injection," he said.

As they spoke of it, the gruesome memory of a recent injection suddenly began to surface in Mary's thoughts. She sat up straight in bed and began to breathe so fast that she was gasping for air. William tried to get her to lie down, but she pushed his hands away. "Oh no, what have I done?" she whispered, her eyes wide with terror. "I thought they were only nightmares—but it was real!"

"What are you saying?" he asked, feeling his own heart pounding rapidly.

Mary turned to him, shaking in fright. "I went to the hospital that night, William! I *was* there! It was gone from my memory until only this moment! Oh dear God, what have I done—I think it was me who killed him!"

Chapter 14

Mary felt her eyelids slowly open. She looked around the room that was now dark except for the light from the fire. William was no longer beside her. Mary tried to sit up.

"Don't try to get up just now, dear," said Abigail's gentle voice from the corner of the room. Mary felt the pillows being straightened behind her head. "You fainted hours ago."

"Where's William?" Mary asked.

"He had to go to the clinic but he should be back shortly," Abigail told her. She handed her a teacup and saucer. "I've made you some chamomile tea."

Mary set the saucer on the nightstand. "Abigail, I may need your promise to take care of Violet…for good."

"Try to rest, Mary," Abigail whispered. "You're not going anywhere."

"I'm afraid I might be going to jail. Did William tell you what happened?"

Abigail poured herself a cup of tea. "There's not a soul in this house who would believe you did any such thing. You must rest and clear your mind now."

William entered the bedroom a few moments later. He placed several bottles of pills on the nightstand. "What are those?" Mary asked.

"They are to help with the pain and help you sleep. We will try only one at a time until we know how your body responds."

"Do you have to get back to the clinic now?"

"I don't have to get back, Mary. The clinic is closed until further notice. I locked the doors and put a sign in the window directing patients to the hospital instead. I'm going to stay here at the house while you recover."

"I remember why I went to the hospital that night," Mary said mournfully. "I'm sorry, William. I should have listened to you about Twilight Sleep. I just wanted to feel what life was like without the pain…I thought it could help me sleep and not hurt so much."

William shook his head. "That's why you never remembered going into the hospital that night."

"I still can't remember all of it," Mary admitted. "I know I went in to ask for the treatment—but I don't know what happened after that. I don't even remember how I got home that night."

"You were just at the wrong place at the wrong time, dear," said Abigail. "If you can't remember what happened, then there is no use worrying about it now."

"Of course I am worried. I was there the same night the doctor turned up dead. I'm worried what I might be truly capable of."

"This is my fault," said William, his voice full of pain. "I should have told you from the beginning why I don't like Twilight Sleep. It's what killed my sister Violet. She had the injection while she was in labor…they tied her to the bed like an animal because she struggled to get away…and she was never the same after that day. The baby did not survive the distress. My sister followed in death not long afterward. I resent that my last memories of her were in such a state. I can't believe you went through that nightmare, Mary. I'm sorry."

There was a knock at the door just then. William opened the door to see Mrs. Spencer. "The detective is here and asks to speak with you, Dr. Hamilton."

William exchanged bewildered glances with Mary and Abigail. "I'll be right there," he said to the housekeeper, then gently closed the door. "Did someone call the police?"

Abigail shook her head. "No one here could have."

"All right—I'll just go downstairs and see what he wants," William tried to say calmly, but the ladies heard the anxiety in his words.

"Abigail, I have to tell them I was there that night," Mary whispered after William left.

"You'll do no such thing."

"What if they suspect William?"

Abigail put her hand over Mary's. "We must pray that is not what's happening downstairs right now." They waited and prayed for William to come through the door and tell them that everything would be all right.

The bedroom door opened slowly, but it wasn't William who came through. It was Ethan. "Abigail, Mary, there you are. William just said to tell Mary not to worry, but he is going down to the police station. What's going on?"

Mary started to cry. Abigail tried to console her. "Now Mary, we don't know that it's anything terrible. He may only be going for a short while as a formality. It does us no use to worry when we don't even know what is happening."

"I want you to call Clara to come here. She deserves to

know what is happening. Please bring her in so I may tell all of you everything."

Clara's mouth hung open as Mary relayed the events of that night, but she did not hesitate to tell Mary exactly what she thought. "Don't even think about trying to turn yourself in, Mary," Clara declared sternly. "Just this morning there was an article in the gossip column—the one I said you wouldn't like—about Dr. Jones and his former cellmate. The convict escaped the prison the same day as the murder. You probably did nothing more than take the injection and go home straight after. The convict could have gotten the doctor after that."

"I wish I could be sure of that, Clara," Mary said. "But the police have my bracelet and who knows what other kind of evidence they may have that I was there. I think it's best to go tell them the truth."

"You mustn't think of doing anything until William comes back," Abigail pleaded. "Mary, you are not well. You're not thinking clearly!"

Mary turned her head to see Violet stirring in the cradle. Mary broke out in tears when she thought of what might happen to her once she walked through the doors of the police station.

Clara turned to leave the room. Ethan stood at the door and opened it for her. "Don't let her leave this room," Clara said. "There's something I have to do." Ethan nodded and closed the door behind her.

Clara went downstairs to the library and sat in front of the telephone at the desk. She made a call to the Yorktown Inn. "Margaret? It's me, Clara. I think you should know what Mary is planning to do."

CHAPTER 15

Phillip Valenti sat at his kitchen table in the early morning hours. He gazed at his mother's ring that seemed so small in his hand.

"Are you getting married, Papa?" Gabriella's voice said from behind him.

Phillip immediately closed his hand over the ring. "I thought you were still sleeping," he said.

"I was, but Donnie kicked me, so now I'm awake." She sat across from him at the table. "Who are you going to give the ring to?" she questioned.

"This is your grandmother's ring. It is very old and has been in the family for many years. She put it in my pocket when I wasn't looking, so I have to return it to her."

"Did Grandma want you to give it to Miss Clara?"

Phillip sighed and evaded the question. "Why would your grandmother do that?"

"Because she saw how pretty and nice Miss Clara is."

Phillip chuckled and opened his hand to show her. "What do you think?"

She gasped at the sight of the ring. "Oh, it's lovely, Papa. Can I keep it?"

He laughed harder this time. "Maybe someday, when you are much much older."

"How much older?"

Phillip shrugged. "Perhaps when you are thirty or forty years old and getting married."

"Thirty or forty!" she exclaimed. "Aren't grownups dead by then?"

"Gabriella Maria," he said, giving her a look. "It's too early for you to be up."

"Are you going to give the ring to Miss Clara?" she persisted.

"Go back to sleep, young lady," he said with a groan. "I will speak to you about it later."

At Davenport House, Mary was getting ready to leave for the police station. Abigail pleaded with her to stay in bed.

"I must know why William never returned last night," Mary said.

"Then let Ethan go to the police station and find out," she urged.

"I need to go and see for myself what is happening, Abigail." Mary took her hat and gloves and left the room.

Clara, Ethan, and Abigail followed her outside and tried to talk her out of it. To everyone's surprise, a car drove up to the house and parked in front, blocking Mary's car from being able to leave. Mrs. Davenport climbed out.

Mary groaned. "What is she doing here?"

Mrs. Davenport walked up to Mary with her new silver cane. "Mary, I've heard what you plan to do and I am here to stop you. I did not work so hard to give you this grand life only for you to throw it all away!"

"You are the last person on earth who could understand what's going on," Mary said.

"What I don't understand is how you could do something so foolish and abandon your family. I've been in jail before, Mary. It is hell on earth and don't think for a second I will let you see inside its walls for as long as I'm alive." The others dared not speak up, for it was the first time they agreed with Mrs. Davenport and hoped that she could convince Mary to listen to her.

"I don't want to go to prison," Mary replied. "I have a paper the police are looking for, and if I don't turn it in, I can never have a clear conscience. It's none of your concern."

Mrs. Davenport stomped her cane into the gravel. "It's every bit of my concern! Who do you think drove you home that night when you could not even walk on your own? Who do you think dressed you in your nightclothes and put you into bed?"

Mary was aghast. "What are you saying?"

"I was there, Mary. My hotel room looks into the windows of the hospital. I watched you go in, and then," she shuddered. "The rest is unspeakable."

"If you know what happened, you must tell me!"

"Trust me, you don't want to hear this," she said, looking around at the others.

"I have to know," said Mary. "It's the only thing I will ever ask of you again!"

Mrs. Davenport looked pained to explain it. She took a reluctant breath before she began. "Dr. Jones grabbed you by the shoulders…I watched as you struggled to get free from his grasp. I remembered the letter you showed me from your mother and I knew what he was capable of. I ran into the hospital just as he was shackling you to a bed by your wrists!

I didn't know what you were doing there or what he had drugged you with. You screamed at him to let you go, and when he did not..." Mrs. Davenport took another deep breath, "...I broke my cane over the back of his head. Then I pulled you out of the hospital as quickly as I could. I thought it best that no one knew we had been there that night. I got rid of my broken cane and took you home."

Mary's heart sank. "You took the page from the register."

Mrs. Davenport breathed in frustration. "I meant to burn that paper, but in my haste I was only concerned about getting you back into the house unnoticed."

No one said a word as they imagined the horror of the situation. They all looked at Mary, who was speechless. Mrs. Davenport finally broke the silence. "Well Mary, now you have something real to tell the police when you go. I certainly wasn't going to stand by and do nothing while my daughter was being tortured by an evil man. But better me than you to go to prison for killing a man. I don't suppose I have much time left anyway."

Mary could not look her in the eye, still feeling uncertain about what to believe. "How did my car get back to the house?"

"I drove you here in it, Mary."

"Then how did you get back to town?"

Mrs. Davenport scoffed. "What do you think? I walked!"

Mary gulped. "It must have been very painful without your cane," she said, though she now wanted to forget the night she tried so hard to remember only hours ago.

"Yes it was," Mrs. Davenport said, wincing from the memory. "Now that I have told you truth of it all, I hope that you would honor a final request from me. I would very much like to see my granddaughter. It's the only chance I will have again."

Mary's lip quivered as she answered her barely above a whisper. "She's upstairs in my room. I will show you to her."

Fiona was astonished when Mary entered the bedroom with Mrs. Davenport. "I'll just go downstairs for a bit," she said quietly, handing Violet to Mary.

Mary turned the baby to face Mrs. Davenport, who seemed to be mesmerized by the sight of her.

"She looks just like you, Mary," she said in wonder. "But what are those marks on her legs?"

Mary looked at Violet and frowned. "They've been there for awhile. I wasn't sure what it was but she seems to be fine."

"Now this is just how you were as an infant. Those are bruises that have never healed. You must take her to the specialists in Philadelphia. If they diagnose her in time, it could save her life."

Mary blinked back tears and nodded. She watched Mrs. Davenport walk over to the nightstand and inspect the bottles of medicine that William brought from the clinic. She held one up in the air for Mary to see. "You mustn't take these, Mary. You are allergic." She set the bottle on the windowsill to set it apart from the others.

Mary looked down at the floor. "Thank you," she said humbly.

Jimmy appeared in the doorway just then. "Grandmother!" he said excitedly, running to hug her.

Mrs. Davenport patted him on the back. Showing affection was never her strong point, but Jimmy did not seem to mind.

"Are you still feeling ill?" he asked.

Mrs. Davenport glanced at Mary then back at Jimmy. "Don't worry about me, dear. Now I have to get back to town. I might be leaving for a long while. I want you to promise to behave yourself and be respectful of your Mistress and every-one else in the house."

"Yes Ma'am," he said. He turned to Mary and smiled. "Now you have met my grandmother! She is the one who told me all about the house."

Mary nodded and managed a smile. She then saw some-thing in his eyes that brought tears to hers. She saw his resem-blance to the man who was a father to her.

Mrs. Davenport left the room and descended the grand staircase for the last time. Clara took her arm and helped her down the stairs with her cane. "I've thought of installing an elevator someday," Clara told her.

Abigail entered Mary's bedroom where Mary still stood in a daze. "Are you just going to let her leave, Mary?" she asked about Mrs. Davenport. "You know that any of us would have done the same if we saw our own child being attacked."

"I know I would have, Abigail," Mary said, drying her eyes with a handkerchief. "I'm so confused—but I think this is the first time in my life that I've understood her as a mother." Perhaps being a mother myself has helped me see."

Abigail took the baby from Mary's arms. "Go to her, Mary. Tell her how you feel."

Mary hurried down the stairs and out the front door. "Wait! Mother!" she called.

Mrs. Davenport turned around to face her. "What is it, Mary?"

Mary wrung her hands together nervously. "There was a time when I thought you belonged in jail, but I believe now that I was mistaken. I am sorry. The police won't hear anything from me about that night."

"What about the rest of them?" Mrs. Davenport asked, pointing to the others with her cane.

"I think they understand that you were doing what you could to protect me," she said quietly. "For all we know, you did save my life that night. When I found out years ago that I was not your real daughter, I was certain you never cared for me. But I see now that you have been trying to help me my whole life, in your own way, as if you were my real mother. I can't say I agree with the way you have done things, but I would still like to hear more from you about the doctor visits from when I was younger. I think I need to know...for Violet's sake as well as my own. Will you come back into the house for tea and we can talk about it?"

"Are you sure?"

Mary nodded. "I'm sure." She took her mother's arm and led her up the stairs to Davenport House.

The telephone in the library was ringing when Mary entered the house. "It might be William," she said to Mrs. Davenport, then hurried to the telephone. "Hello?"

"Mary, thank goodness you're home," William's voice said on the other end. "I telephoned as soon as I could."

"What happened? You've had me worried to death!"

"The police wanted me to help with another body they found. They're attributing both the deaths to an escaped convict in the area."

Mary breathed in relief. "Thank goodness. William, I know that it wasn't me who was responsible for Dr. Jones."

"I never thought it could have been," William answered. "I am glad you believe it for yourself."

"When are you coming home? There is much more to the story that I'd like to tell you."

"I'll be home in a few hours, Mary. I spoke to the hospital director this morning and asked for a change in the contract. I will take the position under the condition that Twilight

Sleep is never offered in my hospital. The director agreed to the change."

Mary felt a wave of peace wash over her. "That's wonderful, William."

"I know it's been a while since I last said this, but I think that everything is going to be all right for us."

Mary smiled. "I think so too. I'll see you soon."

Clara slipped away from the house to visit Phillip Valenti and explain to him all that happened.

Phillip whistled. "There's certainly never a dull moment in the house, is there?"

"Not as long as I've lived in it, at least," she said with a laugh. Then she began to feel shy. "Phillip, I wonder if you might like to come to dinner at the house. Regularly, I mean. The trip to Pittsburgh made me realize how much I enjoy your company and—hope to see you more often."

"I'd like to see you more often too," he admitted.

Clara blushed and looked at the ground. "I'm glad, because I don't want to leave just now," she said.

"You're welcome to stay as long as you'd like, Clara. Always." Phillip fumbled nervously in his pocket while he thought about what to say. "Do you want to see what my mother gave me to give to you?" He showed Clara the family ring.

"Goodness," Clara said, her heart beating wildly. "Does your mother know I'm not Catholic?"

Phillip chuckled. "I told her you weren't, but she still slipped the ring into my pocket when I wasn't looking. I also told her that you don't think of me that way."

Clara stared at him quietly and hoped he would be the first to voice his feelings. She was too nervous to say anything herself. To her relief, Phillip continued, "I keep thinking about that day we spent in Pittsburgh. It felt so nice to be with you that I don't want to send this ring back to my mother. The more I think about it, the more I hope you'll consider wearing it and starting over with me."

Clara covered her red face with her hands.

Phillip grew more serious. "But there is something I need to tell you before you answer. I know you've been betrayed in the past by men who didn't tell you their secrets, but I won't be one of them. Clara, you should brace yourself, because there are only four people in the world who know about this including me, and you'll be the fifth."

Clara nodded solemnly. "I'm listening." Phillip told her his secret, just as he said he would, but Clara could not believe her ears. "I should get back to the house now," she said quietly.

"All right, Clara. I understand if it's too much to think about."

A little while later in the upstairs sitting room, Abigail joined Clara for tea while Mary and Mrs. Davenport occupied the drawing room. "Thank goodness all of that is settled!" Abigail said, sounding exasperated. "Ethan and I are heading back to the manor house now that we know everything will be all right with Mary."

"Abigail, I've been meaning to thank you for helping me when I was suffering from brain fever. You've shown me such kindness throughout all the years since the very day we met. Sometimes I don't know how I could have lived without you."

Abigail beamed. "That's the best compliment anyone has ever paid me. Thank you, Clara. I really hope that you'll come visit us at the manor house sometime. The gardens are exquisite and the house is lovely. I think you would enjoy it."

Clara smiled but seemed to have something pressing on

her mind. "Abigail, can I ask you something? What is it like being married to a Protestant?"

Abigail stifled a giggle. "I suppose I never think of it as being married to a Protestant. I only think of it as being married to Ethan. We are very happy together and Ethan agreed to raise Patrick as Catholic." She noticed Clara's expression change suddenly. "What is it?"

"Phillip told me something—honestly I don't know what to think of it. I wasn't sure if it could be true." She looked Abigail in the eye. "It involves Patrick."

Abigail looked down at her lap and shifted uncomfortably in her seat. She cleared her throat and spoke quietly. "Phillip is a good man. Whatever he said to you—I'm sure was the truth."

"Then you already know what he told me."

Abigail nodded but continued to look at her lap. "Ethan and I can't have any children," she confessed. "We've tried, but the War took everything from us. We must simply remember to keep going no matter how difficult it is at times. And we are grateful to have been blessed with a son before it became impossible for us."

"I see," Clara said gently. "I'm sorry that I had to ask about it, Abigail. I know it was painful for you to say these things just now."

Abigail looked up at Clara. "Phillip must think very highly of you to have confided our situation."

"I suppose we had a chance to bond recently on a trip to Pittsburgh." Clara paused and smiled to remember it. "I met his parents there. The whole time I was visiting his family's house, I thought back to when Phillip asked me to marry him years ago. I regretted that I never gave us a chance, especially now that I know what a good man and father he is. It was wonderful to feel like part of his family—but I wasn't sure what to think when he told me about Patrick. Now that I've spoken to you, I remember the circumstances of those days. I still believe you are two of the most honest and faithful people that I know."

Abigail smiled gratefully. "Thank you for saying so, Clara."

Clara continued in a quiet voice, "And now, after everything that's happened and after all that we've been through, Phillip has asked me to marry him again. Can you believe it?"

Abigail gasped. "Is that why you asked me what it's like to be married to a Protestant?"

Clara felt her face turn pink as she nodded. "I just wondered if it could work—if Phillip could be truly happy with me, and I with him."

"I think the two of you could be very happy indeed," replied Abigail. "Have you answered him yet?"

"Not yet," Clara said with a smile. "But now I know what I'm going to say!"

Abigail laughed when Clara stood up suddenly and exited the sitting room. She knew where Clara was heading.

At the Valenti's farmhouse, Phillip was preparing lunch with the freshly cleaned cook stove. Gabriella was sitting at the table and ready to begin eating, but Donnie sat in front of the window facing the garden. "Papa, Miss Clara is coming again," he said.

"She is?" Phillip hastily washed his hands and left the kitchen to look out the window.

"You forgot to close the firebox!" Gabriella called after him. Phillip turned back to close it but Gabriella beat him to it. "Miss Clara must have distracted you, Papa."

"Thank you for closing it," he said, feeling flustered and embarrassed. "I'm going to change my clothes. Tell Miss Clara that I will be out in a minute, all right?"

She nodded at him. "Are you going to wear your fancy clothes?"

"Yes, Gabriella Maria," he said. "I'm going to wear my fancy clothes."

The children directed Clara to the sofa while she waited. When Phillip emerged from the hallway, he was wearing his suit and had freshly combed hair. He whispered something to his children and they disappeared out the back door. "I'm glad to see you," he said nervously to Clara.

"I'm glad to see you too. I have a question to ask you," Clara said just as nervously.

"Sure, I'm listening," he said.

"I might not be able to have children."

"That wasn't a question," he teased. The playfulness in his voice made Clara feel at ease.

"Does it change your mind?" she asked.

"I'm not going to change my mind, Clara." He opened his hand to reveal the family ring. "Are you going to change yours?"

Clara felt a calming presence settle upon her as she allowed him to slip the ring over her finger. She wondered if it was her mother watching proudly from above. "I'm not going to change my mind, Phillip," she answered. "This is the most certain I've felt about anything in my life."

Epilogue

Jimmy Davenport, Clara's beloved nephew and heir, moved to an upstairs room as one of the family. Mrs. Davenport resigned from her job at the newspaper in order to spend her final days with her grandchildren. Her dying wish to be buried beside her late husband was granted by Clara Valenti, Mistress of the house. Mary, Abigail, Clara, and Serena proudly exercised their right to vote in the presidential election of 1920.

Davenport Estate flourished under the new plans. It went on to become a place of refuge when Hard Times came upon America, just as Mrs. Davenport had forewarned. Jimmy grew up to become known in the community as an honorable man who was always good to his servants...for he followed in the footsteps of the great men and women who went before him at Davenport House.

THE END

From the Author

Blessings to all who have made it with me this far! I am grateful for your time and investment in the lives of these characters who I will dearly miss, now that the series has ended. It is due to your kind support that the Davenport House series grew to be eight books long instead of only the first two. I cannot thank you enough! There were so many twists and turns that sometimes even I did not know where the story was going to go. Some of my favorite scenes were never planned, but rather came to me while I was arranging the chapters. The scene with Clara and Phillip going to Pittsburgh together is one example. The subtleties of this romance seemed to naturally weave their way into the story all along, and I hope you enjoyed how it came together in the end. I wish you well today and always.

Cordially,
Marie Silk

For contact details, exclusive content, and information on upcoming releases, please visit: MarieSilk.com.